DREAMS OF FREEDOM

Challenges of Escaping Dictator Amin's Uganda

By

Evelyn Adlam

About the Book

This is a fiction book based loosely on the story of a brave, determined and resilient girl, who was forced to flee her birth country, Uganda, and she was allowed to settle in the United Kingdom. Her escape was during the brutal rule of Idi Amin Dada, the then Uganda's president, who ruled the country from 1971 to 1986, with an iron fist. But little did she know that she would encounter many more major challenges in the years ahead. However, resilient as she had become, she triumphed over almost all of them.

The names depicted in the book are fictional, apart from Idi Amin Dada's names.

Acknowledgment

My compliments go, first and foremost, to my beloved husband, Ian James Howarth, who has given me his full support and encouragement throughout this project. Whenever I've been engrossed in writing the book, he has not complained about being left to handle most of the household duties, and as both of us are keen cooks, he has not minded spending a lot of time in the kitchen; he's always made sure that there is food on the table at all mealtimes.

My grateful thanks also go to the Writers Clique team, particularly Adam Smith, the Project Manager; Anne Quinn and Viona Davis, the Editors, all of whom have given me immeasurable support throughout the project and have guided me through the complicated maze of writing and producing this, my first, fiction book. Without their assistance, the task would have been much more extraneous.

A very big thank you to them all.

TABLE OF CONTENTS

CHAPTER 1

EVENTFUL DEPARTURE

Helen Mwanga cautiously walked into the departure lounge of Entebbe Airport and nervously looked around the room to find somewhere to sit in the poorly lit room. It was a cold, gloomy and wet morning, and many of the ceiling lights were out of order, which was hardly surprising considering the economic state of Uganda at that time.

She walked slowly towards an unoccupied bench at the end of the room and sat down. She kept looking around her to see if any of the many army soldiers roaming around the room, with rifles over their shoulders, were interested in her at all. None of them seemed to be interested in her. She held her black leather bag tightly on her lap with her hands trembling; she had nothing else with her. She felt lonely and was now even starting to get nauseous. As she anxiously waited for the announcement of her plane's embarkation, she continuously looked around the room to make sure that she was not attracting anyone's attention.

After a while, she noticed two catholic nuns coming through the entrance, and they were looking around for somewhere to sit. By now, the departure lounge was getting quite full. They walked towards where she was sitting, and noticing that there were empty spaces at her bench, one of the nuns walked quickly towards her and said to her: "Do you mind if we sat here with you?"

"I don't mind. Please go ahead," Helen replied, with a gentle smile. The nun smiled back and thanked her.

"I'm Sister Maria," one of the nuns said, "and this is Sister Martha," pointing at her colleague. "Nice to meet you," Sister Maria said, as the two Sisters sat down beside Helen and placed their hand luggage on the floor by their side of the bench.

"And your name is?" Sister Maria asked.

"My name is Helen Mwanga," Helen said. "I'm pleased to meet you, Sisters."

The Sisters had travelled the previous week from a Catholic convent in Nairobi, Kenya, to attend a Christian conference in Kampala, Uganda.

◆═══◆

They were now due to fly back to Nairobi on the same flight Helen also was booked on. They'd had a very busy time at the conference, and they were looking forward to getting back to their less hectic life at the Convent in Nairobi.

"You seem a bit nervous, Helen," Sister Maria said, "what's the matter? Does flying make you anxious?"

"I'm alright, Sister," replied Helen. "Honestly, I'm fine, and I'm not bothered with flying."

"That's fine then, Helen," continued Sister Maria. "Let's hope the flight will be on time."

As the Sisters were getting themselves comfortable on the bench, Helen could vaguely see a smartly dressed gentleman at the far end of the departure lounge. He was walking towards the side of the departure lounge where she and the Sisters were sitting. She couldn't immediately work out who he was, but she thought he had familiar mannerisms in the way he walked. 'Could that be my boss at work?' she thought. 'That will be a disaster.' She was getting more nervous and anxious as he got closer. She, however, hoped and prayed that it was not who she thought was. As the man drew closer, Helen clearly noticed that it was, indeed, her immediate boss at work, Benjamin Okuri. He was the head of the Finance Department at Uganda Produce Holdings (UPH), where she worked. 'This will be terrible!' she further thought.

Benjamin Okuri was a close friend of the then President of Uganda, Idi Amin, so close to the President that the President had also appointed him to the President's spy unit, the General Service Unit (GSU). This unit was empowered to spy on the public during their day-to-day activities, and report any perceived misgivings back to the President, for him to decide what to do with the people involved. Many prominent people were wrongly reported to the President as being against him. In many cases the President had decided that they should be killed for objecting to his rule.

At UPH, Ben Okuri's fellow employees were weary of his spying activities, but there was not much they could do about it: they just avoided his company as much as they could. It was also an open secret that President Amin had ordered his appointment as head of the Finance Department at UPH where Helen worked as a Senior Accountant. Therefore, she knew, for sure, that Ben Okuri, being her immediate boss, and member of the GSU, would take it extremely seriously if he discovered that she was travelling out of the country without his knowledge. She quietly, but very nervously, watched him making his way through the crowd of passengers towards where she and the two Sisters were sitting.

Ben Okuri recognised Helen from a distance: he then walked quickly towards her and when he got to her, he stood still and, looking straight into her eyes, and in a loud and angry voice, he said: "Helen, where are you travelling to? How come I didn't know about it before now?"

Helen, pretending to be very confident, jumped from her seat, and looking back at him with a brave stare, said: "Sir, I'm not travelling anywhere; I'm here just to see these Sisters off. I was very sure that I'd get back before the offices opened; that's why I didn't mention it to you. I'll get back to the office as soon as the Sisters have departed, Sir."

Ben Okuri then turned to the Sisters and said politely: "How're you Sisters? It's very nice to meet you. I wish you a pleasant and safe journey."

Turning back to Helen, he said: "I'll be back in the office this afternoon, and I hope to continue discussing with you the projects I allocated you, and which you're currently working on. Don't be late."

◆═══◆

He waved goodbye to the Sisters and walked away hurriedly.

The Sisters looked at each other in surprise, and then at Helen, and Sister Maria said: "What was that all about?"

Helen nervously turned round, looked at them, and softly whispered: "Quiet, please! It's a very long story and it's quite complicated. I'll tell you later."

She looked all around her again, and very quietly, she continued saying to the Sisters: "I hope I'll manage to get away today safely and in one piece!" They noticed that she was shaking all over. "I'll tell you everything when we're safely in the air. I hope you understand." Her lips were quivering, and there were tears in her eyes.

"Oh, dear child," said Sister Maria, as she got up. She pulled Helen up from the bench and continued: "Please get closer to us; in fact, come and sit between us. We'll do our best to protect you!" The two Sisters moved slightly and made room for her between them. They then put their hands around Helen and gave her a comforting hug. Sister Maria then said: "Don't worry, young lady.

We'll pray hard for your safety, won't we, Sister Martha?"

"Of course we will," Sister Martha said emphatically.

Not long after that, a loud announcement was made, asking all the passengers travelling to Nairobi to proceed to board the plane through Gate 3. The Sisters held Helen's hands tightly as they moved through Gate 3 to go up the steps to the plane. Inside the plane, Sister Maria requested the flight attendant to let the three of them sit together in the plane, and the attendant said she would do her best to do that. She asked them to follow her as she led them to three seats towards the back of the plane, by the window.

"I hope these seats will be okay for you," the attendant said with a gentle smile. "Enjoy your flight," she continued, and then walked away. The Sisters put Helen between them and tried to make sure she was comfortable and relaxed.

"Feeling comfy, Helen?" asked Sister Maria as she pulled out a book from her hand luggage to read during the flight.

"Very comfortable, thank you very much, Sister," answered Helen. "You've both been very kind to me." She then leaned back into her seat and closed her eyes, ready for a little nap. Sister Martha, too, did the same.

While the plane was still stationary on the ground, an announcement came via the plane's loudspeaker: "Before we can take off, Will the following people please identify themselves? If you hear your name, please report to the security personnel at the front of the plane."

Helen sat up quickly and looking at each Sister, she said: "There we go!" she said. "My name is on that list, without a doubt! That boss of mine must have already found out that I was leaving the country, and he'd want to teach me a lesson! He would never miss a chance like this!"

"My dear girl," said Sister Martha. "You're not yet sure about that! "Let's wait to hear the names on the list."

Both Sisters put their hands around Helen and cuddled her tightly. Helen was now sobbing heavily, and tears were falling onto her lap. The Sisters closed their eyes and waited anxiously to hear the names being read out.

A bulky army man in an army uniform came from the cockpit area and stood at the front of the plane, holding the list in his hand. Sturdily, he read out the names: Gordon Nsubuga, Boniface Okot, Joyce Mayanja, Olivia Were, Elizabeth Auma, Musa Olimu, Michael Tabule, Davis Mukasa, and a few more others. When he finished reading out the names, he went back into the cockpit.

With her head against Sister Martha's shoulder, Helen shut her eyes and covered her face with her hands and wept softly. She couldn't even bear listening to the names as they were being read out. But she had convinced herself that her name would be on the list. When the army man came to the end of the list, he folded the paper and asked the identified people standing in front of him to follow him out of the plane.

Unsure of what was happening, Helen continued to cry, shaking her head from side to side. After a while, it all went quiet. She raised her head to look into Sister Martha's eyes, and she whispered: "Is that the end of the list? Was my name read out?"

"No, no, no!" exclaimed both Sisters in unison. "Your name wasn't on the list!" continued Sister

Maria. "Cheer up, girl, sit up and let's enjoy the flight!" The two Sisters again cuddled her tightly. And the plane started moving forward slowly, then faster, and up it went, on its way to Nairobi!

Helen, who had by now cheered up a little, sat straight, wiped away her tears, and with a faint smile, turned first to Sister Maria, then to Sister Martha, and then put her arms around both, and with a big smile, she said: "I can't believe I'm getting away! Hurray!"

Without saying anything, Sister Maria pulled Helen lovingly towards her and gave her another big hug.

"Now I seriously need a nap," Helen said. "I hope there will be no further drama! I can now close my eyes for a well-earned nap." She went to sleep straight away, and the rest of the flight to Nairobi was uneventful.

Upon disembarking at Nairobi airport, the two Sisters held Helen's hands as they walked out. "Let's go out and look for somewhere to sit," Sister Maria said to Helen. "You can then tell us your amazing story. We can't wait to hear it!"

"That's okay with me," answered Helen as the three of them continued walking towards a bench in a small garden nearby. They all sat down comfortably on the bench, and amidst tears, Helen related her story to the Sisters, The Sisters were completely stunned!

CHAPTER 2

LIFE IN OLD AND NEW UGANDA

When Helen was growing up, Uganda was a beautiful, prosperous country with a glorious temperate climate all the year round, and it was almost always green and lush in the southern part of Uganda, where she was born and grew up. The capital of Uganda, Kampala, was the closest town to her home, and Lake Victoria was a short drive away. At that time, Kampala was extremely vibrant, with successful businesses everywhere going on all day long. The nightlife too was vibrant; there were always exciting and buzzing restaurant/dance venues to go to.

Whilst at university, Helen and her friends and colleagues truly enjoyed the city's vibrant restaurants of various cuisines from different parts of the world, as well as its numerous nightclubs. At most weekends, they loved visiting the nightclub closest to the university, the Susanna Nightclub, where they enjoyed the vigorous dancing to all sorts of music. Due to its amazing beauty and greenery, Sir Winston Churchill, one of the most famous prime ministers of the United Kingdom, called Uganda 'The Pearl of Africa.'

While many African countries were colonies of Britain, Uganda was a British protectorate. As such, Uganda did not experience the kind of harsh rule and other habits that followed it, such as racism, which many of the colonies did. Helen, therefore, grew up in a friendly, multi-racial environment, where different races lived quite happily together. The children of different races mingled very well together. Whilst at primary school, Helen's two best friends were from two different races: a British girl called Frances Wilson, and an Asian girl called Zaina Mehta. The three girls always played together, and often visited each other's homes. Even after leaving primary school, they remained firm friends, and they even kept in touch with each other as adults.

Helen adored her university time. She attended Makerere University College, which was then the only university for the whole of East Africa, and she studied economics. She happily made friends with students of different races, as well as many coming from different tribes of Uganda, Kenya, and Tanzania. The students worked hard at their studies, and they also enjoyed taking part in the university's social activities, which were held mostly in the evenings and weekends. As the university was fully residential, many students had plenty of time to make lifelong friends, several of them eventually getting married after graduating.

Helen, too, was attracted to a fellow student, Steven Rugara, a Law student who was born and grew up in Mbarara, Ankole, Western Uganda, which was a long distance from Kampala, Southern Uganda, where Helen was from, and where the university was situated.

Ordinarily in Uganda, most families preferred their children to befriend or marry people from their own regions, or even tribes. So, Helen and Steven's friendship was not expected to last. But Helen and Steven proved the doubters wrong: they became extremely close friends, and they were also pleasantly surprised when their families did not object to their relationship and giving them their blessings. By the time Helen and Steven got to their second year at university, they had become serious boyfriend and girlfriend, and they were now almost inseparable. They also tended to spend most of their free time together, such as lunch and dinner times, at the university canteen and other such places.

Steven couldn't always go home to Mbarara for short college breaks. So, quite often he would spend such breaks at Helen's family's home, and his and Helen's parents did not object to him doing so.

Helen and Steven graduated from Makerere University in the 1969/1970 academic year, Helen with first-class degree in Economics and Steven a first-class degree in Law. The two sets of parents proudly attended their graduation ceremony. After the ceremony, Steven's father took the two families out for a celebratory meal at a lovely restaurant in Kampala city. It was a joyous occasion, and the attendees, indeed, let their hair down. The two graduating youngsters felt very lucky and blessed to have such loving and caring parents.

There was, however, a change of government in Uganda in 1971 when the Army, led by Corporal Idi Amin, staged a coup, overthrowing the legally elected government. Idi Amin immediately declared himself President of Uganda, Commander-in-Chief of the Armed Forces, Uganda Army Chief of Staff and Chief of Air Staff.

He ruled the country as if it was his personal property; he appointed his family and friends to jobs in various government organisations, and he also directed Chief Executives of private corporations and companies to employ his relatives and friends. Anybody opposing him was arrested and summarily imprisoned or 'made to disappear' (to be killed on the orders of Idi Amin – the term Ugandans used to avoid being punished by the new Government)! President Amin also created the spying unit, the General Service Unit (GSU) soon after staging the coup.

Idi Amin transformed Uganda into a Police State, and the people in the country were now living in constant fear. If anybody in a particular profession 'upset' him in any way, Idi Amin would put the blame on all members of that profession. For instance, if a medical doctor disagreed with him on

something, the President would blame the whole
medical profession, and he would order the
detention of many senior doctors, many of whom
would be 'made to disappear'. On one occasion, a
well-known lawyer had an argument with the
President, and as a result, several lawyers 'were
made to disappear'. Such punishments also befell
other professions. These 'disappearances' caused
many Ugandan professionals in different
professions to flee the country to work abroad,
resulting in a major brain drain.

 The situation in Uganda after Idi Amin came to
power was such a change from what most Ugandans
had been used to. The casual, carefree living that
was there previously turned into a 'survival of the
fittest' mode. There were shortages of everything in
the country: services, food, fuel, utilities, etc., and
the currency was extremely devalued, making it
very difficult for people to purchase anything.

Helen and Steven graduated barely a year
before Idi Amin came to power. As they were eager
to secure employment soon after leaving university,
they sent off job applications to various government
ministries and private sector companies during their
last few weeks at university. With the good degrees
they obtained, both of them were lucky to secure

jobs in Kampala quite quickly. Helen joined the Uganda Produce Holdings (UPH) as a Junior Accountant and was placed on a six-month probation. Steven joined the Uganda Ministry of Legal Affairs (ULA) as a Junior Lawyer, also on a probation of six months.

Helen's immediate boss was Ben Okuri, who was from the same Northern Uganda region as Idi Amin. At the start, Ben Okuri was a nice boss to Helen: he was very helpful and a good mentor. But when Idi Amin came to power and appointed him to the GSU, Ben Okuri changed somehow. He was not as committed to his UPH job as he was before, and he was away from his office often, supposedly to carry out his GSU duties. However, he was still quite impressed with Helen's work, and at the end of her probationary period he confirmed her in her position, and soon after that recommended her for promotion to the position of Senior Accountant.

Steven, too, was doing very well at ULA, where his work was greatly appreciated; he was also confirmed in his position at the end of his six-month probation. Both Helen and Steven were very pleased with their work progress, and they took pride in going to work every day.

Both UPH and ULA provided housing for their staff, and therefore both Helen and Steven were entitled to housing in Kampala, provided by their employers. They, however, preferred the accommodation provided by UPH, and so they decided to make that their first home together. They moved in just before Christmas, and they turned it into a beautiful and comfortable apartment. They, both adored it tremendously.

Despite the drastic change in the governance of Uganda, Helen's workplace, UPH, continued to be a pleasant and friendly environment, and she loved being part of it. She made friends with many of her work colleagues, her closest being Betty Mukasa, Martin Oboo and Joseph Magara who occupied the offices closest to hers. Very often they went together to the work canteen after work for a drink or two.

Steven also became quite friendly with Helen's work colleagues, and he often joined them at UPH's canteen after work. Helen, however, used to work late, and quite often she went to the canteen after Steven had arrived and was already having a drink with her workmates. Steven thoroughly enjoyed the company of Helen's work colleagues, as well as their lively discussions. He felt very comfortable there.

Martin Oboo told Helen and some of his other close friends at UPH, in confidence, that he was President Amin's nephew: his mother was Idi Amin's sister. He, however, assured them that his close relationship with President Amin would not change his relationship with them. He kept his word: he never bragged to them about his relationship with the President. As such, nobody at UPH was bothered about his identity, to them he was just a very nice and sociable person. Helen and her work colleagues considered him a wonderful guy, who was always friendly and very helpful.

One Friday evening, Helen walked into a crowded canteen, and as always, Steven was already there having a drink with her friends and colleagues. He quickly got up and ran to her. "Hello, darling!" he said, putting his arms around her and giving her a kiss. Before they sat down, he said to her: "Darling, we're going to have the party, which, as you'll remember, we said we'd have on a boat on Lake Victoria!" And before Helen said anything, Steven continued: "I think we should hold it in two weeks' time. What do you say?" While Helen was trying to recall the conversation, Steven continued: "I apologise, but I've already discussed it with your friends and colleagues here, and they all appear quite enthusiastic about, and supportive of it!" He then looked directly at Helen's best mates, Martin Oboo and Joseph Magara, and said: "Isn't that so?"

Helen was quite surprised; she took a nervous step back and looked directly into Steven's eyes, and then broke into a big smile and said: "Oh yes, darling, I now remember! But why so soon? There is a lot of work we need to do before we can hold the party, and it's going to be expensive as you know. What's the rush?"

"I don't think it's a rush, darling," Steven answered calmly. "Many of your friends and colleagues here are very excited about it, and, regarding the expenses, many have offered to assist with the cost and the preparations. Isn't that great?"

"Yes, yes!" Martin shouted, as he jumped off his seat. "It's quite a unique idea, and I reckon it will be the first such party held on Lake Victoria! I bet it'll be the best party ever held in Kampala!"

Helen turned round and looked at the group and, after a few seconds, gave them a wide smile. She ran towards them and put her hands around Martin and Joseph and said: "Okay, we'll do it and, of course, with all your help, it's going to be an amazing party. Let's all be determined to make it so!" Holding Steven's hand tightly and looking in his eyes, she continued: "Can we therefore ask these wonderful friends of ours to come over to our place for a meeting next weekend to go through what needs to be done, and how we're going to go about everything? Yes?"

"Yes!" answered all their friends in unison. "Till next weekend, then," said Joseph.

The following Saturday, many of Helen's and Steven's friends gathered at their apartment and discussed what needed to be done and divided themselves into sub-groups to do the different jobs. Martin was designated as the Master of Ceremonies and tasked with supervising the music. Betty Mukasa was put in charge of the food, and Joseph would oversee the drinks. Everyone accepted the tasks they were assigned, and they all promised to do their best to make the party a very successful event. The party was scheduled to be held on the Sunday two weeks from then. The invitations were sent out to members of the two families who lived in Kampala and its environs, close friends, and work colleagues at both Steven's and Helen's places of work.

Early on the day of the Party, guests started arriving at Lake Victoria Beach quite early in the morning. They were guided to their seats on the boat by Martin, the Master of Ceremonies. A band and dancing space were located at the front of the boat, and the band had already started playing soft music. At the back of the boat, Betty and Joseph had laid out the food and drinks on two large tables. Betty and her small team responsible for the food kept the food warm on portable stoves laid along the table.

Once all the guests were comfortably seated, relishing their food and the music, the boat gracefully began cruising along the lake. The stunning views of the shoreline left the guests feeling truly indulged!

After the guests had finished their meal, the band started playing lively dance music, and many of the guests took to the floor to dance, filling up all the space closest to the band, which was allocated for dancing. Both adults and children were on the dance floor enjoying themselves. It was a jolly and enjoyable scene to watch!

After a while, Steven asked the band to play one of his and Helen's favourite songs quietly. He then said to the guests: "Can you all please sit down? I have something to say."

The guests left the dance floor and went back to their seats. Steven then took Helen's hand and led her to the middle of the empty dance floor. He went down on one knee in front of her and extended his hand towards her, holding a small white box, containing an engagement ring. He said: "Helen darling, will you marry me?"

It was very unusual of Steven to keep secrets from her, and, therefore, Helen was speechless! This was, indeed, a big surprise to her. Tears started running down her cheeks! She stood there like a statue, not knowing what to say. This was truly a big secret Steven had kept from her until then. "Please, please answer me!" he nervously pleaded. The guests jumped to their feet and, in unison, chanted: "Please, Helen, say yes, yes, yes!"

Helen, now a little composed, looked round the room for reassurance and, with a big smile on her face, finally answered: "Yes, yes, darling Steven, of course, I'll marry you!" And she moved close to him and gave him a big kiss on the lips, and they embraced fondly. The guests clapped loudly and wildly cheered them! The band then played the song more loudly, which was an invitation to Helen and Steven to lead the guests in a slow romantic dance. It was a magical moment and a time of great joy for the two lovers and all their guests. The joyful party went on until late in the evening.

When Helen went back to work on the Monday following the boat party, she was surprised to find out that news of her engagement to Steven had already circulated throughout UPH, and many colleagues who she encountered congratulated her warmly. Even her immediate boss, Ben Okuri, was so thrilled to hear her good news that he went to her office and gave her a big and long hug. The Chief Executive of UPH, Isaac Bukenya, too, had heard the news, and he also came to her to give her his special congratulations. He patted her on the back and said to her: "Helen, if you need any help with the wedding arrangements, please do not hesitate to ask. We'll be happy to help."

Helen gave Mr. Bukenya a big smile and said: "That's very kind of you. I appreciate your kind offer very much, Sir."

When she was left alone in her office, she couldn't believe that many of her work colleagues were genuinely pleased with her news. She quietly settled at her desk, closed her eyes, and attempted to absorb it all. She said to herself: "I'm so blessed to have all this at this point of my life: a good job, wonderful work colleagues, and a gorgeous and loving fiancé." She raised her hands in prayer and said: "Thank you, Lord!"

Many of her colleagues said to her that she deserved everything she got as she was always there for them and always gave a helping hand to them when they needed it. They were all genuinely very happy for her.

With the engagement out of the way, Helen and Steven now turned their attention to the wedding preparations. They decided that the wedding would take place in four months' time from then. They realised that as they both belonged to relatively large extended families, the wedding was going to be a big one, and as such, they would need to do a lot of preparations. However, as a lot of family members and friends had already volunteered to help, the load would not be too daunting. So, more meetings were held at Helen and Steven's home to discuss what had to be done on the actual day of the wedding.

Helen's older brother, Philip, took charge of allocating and coordinating all the tasks to be done on the day, and he promptly appointed sub-groups to carry out the various tasks. All those appointed started their jobs right away. For the next couple of Sundays, the volunteers attended further meetings at Helen and Steven's home to report on the progress of their tasks. It was confirmed that the wedding would be held at All Saints Church in Kampala, Uganda's capital city.

One major task remaining for Helen and Steven was to take a trip to Steven's parents in Mbarara, Western Uganda to verify with them the last details of the wedding arrangements, including their journey to Kampala, and their accommodation there. So, Helen and Steven planned the trip to Mbarara to take place on the following Friday. They planned to leave Kampala for Mbarara on that Friday evening after work. Helen applied for a day's leave for that Friday as she wanted to pack their luggage for the trip well in advance of Steven coming home after work. She expected Steven to arrive home by 5.00 pm so that they could start their drive to Mbarara before dark. By 4.00 pm, Helen had already packed their cases and was just waiting for Steven to arrive from work so that they could set off for Mbarara soon. She was very excited!

By 5.00 pm, Steven hadn't returned, and Helen was getting quite anxious. 'Maybe he has an urgent job to finish off at the office,' she thought. 'I would give him a few more minutes before I phone him.' She waited, waited and waited, but Steven was nowhere to be seen; he had not even phoned her to tell her what was causing the delay. When it got to 5.45 pm, Helen thought: 'This is so unlike Steven, he's always a meticulous timekeeper. I better phone him at his office.' So, she telephoned his office. The office secretary, Sarah, answered the call.

"Hi Sarah, this is Helen," she said. "Can you please put me through to Steven?"

"Oh, gracious me, Helen!" Sarah exclaimed. "You obviously haven't yet heard! Earlier this afternoon, Steven was taken away by army soldiers, but we don't know why or where he's been taken."

"What?" Helen screamed into the phone. "By whom? By the army, you said?"

"Yes, Helen, by the army," Sarah confirmed. "Could have been by the GSU, the President's General Service Unit, but we're not sure, and we don't know where he's been taken or what for. That's why we're still here in the office waiting to see if we can get any information or see him brought back. We don't know what to do next. We're very, very confused, Helen!"

"I can't believe this!" Helen exclaimed. "But thank you for letting me know, Sarah," Helen said as she put down the phone.

'I can't believe this has happened to Steven!' she was thinking loudly, amid loud sobs. "Steven would be the last person on earth to be arrested by the

Secret Service. What would they take him for? I'm going to go now to the 'Command Post' (President Amin's residence) to find out why my Steve has been taken away, what is the reason behind this, and where he's been taken to! It's just not fair."

Without any hesitation, Helen ran downstairs, with tears streaming down her cheeks, got into her car and drove like crazy towards President Amin's Command Post. She just wanted to find out from the highest power in the land where her fiancé was and why he'd been taken away. 'I must do so before it is too late,' she said to herself. She knew that Steven would not have a chance of surviving the horrible treatment that the people arrested by the GSU were subjected to. She drove at break-neck speed towards the Command Post.

She reached the Command Post in less than ten minutes. She stopped the car with a loud squeak a few metres from the main entrance and jumped out. The army soldiers guarding the entrance put their hands up towards her to stop her as she was walking speedily towards the gate.

"Stop, stop, young lady," one of the guards, with a loaded gun over his shoulder, shouted. "Who do you think you are, and where do you think you are going?"

◆═════◆

"I want to see the President quickly to ask him where my fiancé, Steven Rugara, has been taken by the GSU," answered Helen very loudly. "Why was he arrested this afternoon? Where is he now? That's what I want to know!"

"The President won't be able to help you," said the guard. "It sounds like a Police matter. That's where you need to go. It's not a matter for the President at all. You must leave immediately!"

"But I want to speak to the President," Helen shouted back, loudly and in a wailing voice. "I'm sure he'll be able to tell me where his men have taken my fiancé. I want my fiancé back!" Crying very loudly now, Helen fell to her knees, and with a river of tears running down her face, she screamed: "It's very urgent for, and very important to, me!"

It was now late afternoon. Helen could see in the distance, at the front door of the main building of Command Post, President Amin walking out to the front porch. He then shouted: "Who's that, and what do they want?"

"It's a young lady, Sir; we don't know her name yet," answered the guard. "She says she wants to speak to you urgently, Your Excellency."

"That's okay, said the President. "Let her come in. If she wants to speak to me, I'll see her."

"Very well, your Excellency. We'll let her through," said the guard. Turning to Helen, he said: "You can go through now. The President will see you." Helen walked speedily towards the Command Post's front door. There were army personnel standing close to the President, with guns slang over their shoulders. But they were polite, and some of them even said hello to Helen. She finally was standing directly in front of President Amin at very close range. She couldn't believe how tall, big, and broad he was. She stood like a statue and stared at him in amazement. "Hello, Your Excellency," she mumbled.

"Hello to you too," said the President, bending slightly to be able to get down to her height. "What is your name, and what did you say you want to see me about?" asked President Amin quietly but firmly.

"Mr. President, thank you for agreeing to see you at such short notice," Helen said nervously, shaking, and with tears running down her cheeks: "Your Excellency, my name is Helen Mwanga. I have come directly to you because I believe you are the best person to tell me where my fiancé, Steven Rugara, is being held. He was collected by armed army soldiers from his office this afternoon, by GSU soldiers, but the soldiers did not say where they were taking him or for what reason. Surely, Your Excellency, you must be able to tell me something."

Helen fell to her knees and wailed uncontrollably. "Please, please, Your Excellency, I beg you to help me! Steven and I are engaged and we're due to get married soon. Wedding plans are already under way; without him, obviously, the wedding won't take place. Please, please, help me, your Excellency. I beg you!"

President Amin took Helen's hand, pulled her to her feet, and said: "Come with me inside the house, young lady. We'll sit down indoors and have a chat. Okay?" He led her to a private reception room inside the Command Post. "Sit down here with me," he said to her, patting the space next to him. There was nobody else present in the room and this made Helen quite nervous. Despite her body still shaking, she sat down next to President Amin, wiped away her tears, and loudly blew her nose. She looked directly into President Amin's eyes and said: "Your Excellency, my fiancé, Steven Rugara, is the most innocent man I know; he would never hurt anybody, and everybody knows that." After a little pause, she continued: "Can you please tell me where you ordered him to be taken? He needs to be rescued before anything horrible happens to him."

"Did you say your name is Helen, young lady?" the President asked softly. "Now, Helen, I'll tell you something."

Helen sat up straight, fixed her eyes on the President and said eagerly: "Yes? Your Excellency, please, please do. You can see I'm eagerly waiting!"

The President placed his hand over Helen's shoulder and said: "My dear girl, you shouldn't listen to people who are telling horrible lies about me. I never, and I repeat never, ordered your fiancé's arrest. Many, many bad people tell all sorts of lies about me; they just want to create confusion in the country, the country I'm desperately trying to govern peacefully. It's very wrong of them to do so, don't you think so? Please don't listen to them or believe them."

He then continued, "But don't worry, I'll see what I can do to help you. I'm going to ask my Minister of Internal Affairs to investigate this case for you immediately, and I'll ask him to tell me the full story as soon as possible. Then, I'll ask him to contact you right away to let you know the findings. Is that alright?"

"Yes, Your Excellency," Helen said. "I'll appreciate that very much, thank you. I'll be eagerly waiting." The President walked towards the corner of the room where a few telephone sets were. The phones were of different colours, and the President picked the red one and dialed the Minister of Internal Affairs, Henry Kwach. Over the phone, the President said to the Minister in his native language: "There's a young woman here I need you to thoroughly investigate. She claims she's come to me looking for answers about her fiancé, who she says was taken by my soldiers. I've never heard of the man she's talking about. I'm not sure if she's been sent by my enemies to gather information or to scope out the Command Post for their own malicious purposes.

"Can you dig up everything you can on, and whoever may have sent, her? If she's playing us, she will face serious consequences for her actions. While you are with her, I'll also be conducting my own investigation. We can't afford to let her slip away if she's here under false pretenses."

While waiting, Helen got up and went to look at some photographs on the walls. There was army paraphernalia thrown about the room, and she had to carefully dodge the pieces. Slowly she got to the photographs. Most of them were about Army scenes with President Amin as the focal point. She looked at some of them with interest. She noticed one photograph which contained Idi Amin shaking hands with the previous President of Uganda, who he overthrew some months ago, and they were both smiling widely at each other. Helen laughed quietly and thought: 'Why is President Amin keeping a photograph where his enemy is displayed so prominently? I wonder if this is his way of deceiving people, giving them the impression that they were his friends who he cared for just before he turned against them. Will he do the same to me? I wonder.' She walked on and looked at a few more photographs, and then walked back to the sofa and sat down. When she saw the President walking back, she immediately straightened herself and waited eagerly for what he was going to say to her.

The President stood in front of her and then roughly pulled her from the sofa and towards him. Helen's head came just to his stomach. She tried to look up him in the eyes, but his big tummy was in the way; she fell back onto the sofa. The President pulled her up again, bent down to get close to her face and said to her: "I've spoken to the Minister about your fiancé, and I've asked him to come over immediately to take you with him and to see what he can do to help you find him. He'll be here shortly."

Within a few minutes, the Minister arrived, and the President gave him instructions, again in their native language, and Helen wondered if the President was telling his minister not to do anything with Steven's case, having heard about many similar cases before. The President turned to Helen and said: "This is my Minister of Internal Affairs, Henry Kwach. He'll assist you with looking for your fiancé, and I'm sure we'll shortly get news of his whereabouts. Okay, young lady?"

"That's fine, your Excellency. Thank you very much," Helen responded. The Minister then led Helen out of the room.

THE KILLING ROOMS

When they left the President's residence, the Minister, Henry Kwach, stood still for a while, thinking hard about how he was going to handle Helen. He carefully considered the best way to extract the information the President wanted. He said to himself: 'I think I'll take her to the detention centres to see what her reaction will be; I think from her mannerism as we go round the centres, I'll get an idea of who she is and what her intentions are. Yes, I'll do that.'

He turned to Helen and said: "Please follow me; we'll go first to the detention centres, just in case your friend was taken there by mistake; occasionally, and I mean very occasionally, this happens to some people. Let's see what we can find. You must trust me."

He led her to a building next door to the Command Post, and they entered through a side door and down a long, dark and scruffy corridor. Midway down the corridor, they came to a heavily bolted door, with a large padlock on it. The Minister pulled out a bunch of keys from his pocket, flipped through them, and eventually he found the right key for the door. He opened it and asked Helen to follow him inside. As soon as they stepped into the room, a nasty stench immediately engulfed them. The smell was so intoxicating that Helen placed her hand over her nose and mouth. She turned to the minister and said: "Sir, the room smells so awful, and not fit for human beings! Are you sure we're in the right place?"

"Yes, of course, it is the right place, young lady," Henry Kwach replied. "It's not supposed to be a hotel. It is a detention centre, for heaven's sake! It is where troublesome people are brought. But as I said to you, some innocent people are brought here by mistake occasionally. I'd wondered whether your friend could have been brought here, or taken to another centre, by mistake."

As they walked on, Henry Kwach said to Helen: "As we go round the room, can you look at the faces of the people to see if one of them is your friend, sorry, your fiancé? If we don't find him here, then we will go to another location."

The room was dimly lit, but Henry Kwach had brought a torch with him, which he switched on then. "Please continue to look at all the faces carefully," he said to her.

As they walked forward, Helen noticed that most of the people had gunshot wounds. Some people were limbless, and others had their eyes gouged out. Many of them were stark-naked, and almost all were covered in blood, and she could see a few bodiless heads! The biggest shock, though, was to see dead bodies left lying on the floor amongst those still alive!

Many of those people still alive were huddled together, crying and groaning weakly. From time to time, the minister stopped to turn some of the people's faces towards Helen, asking her if any of them were her fiancé's. But Helen's answer was always: "No!"

It was a gruesome picture, and Helen almost fainted! She, however, kept going, telling herself: 'Helen, please be brave for the sake of your beloved fiancé, Steven!'

Finally, they got to the end of the room, and turning to Helen, the minister said: "It appears we haven't found your fiancé here. We'll have to try elsewhere." He then led her out of the room.

When they got outside, Helen was feeling sick and nauseated. She stopped walking and suddenly got violently sick on the lawn. Whilst still bent down, she quietly said to the minister: "I'm very sorry about this, Sir, but being inside that horrible room was overwhelming! I'm sorry I couldn't stop myself from getting sick."

The minister patted her on the back and said: "I'm sorry you felt that bad, dear girl. As you get badly affected, I guess you wouldn't like to continue the search. There's one other place I would have wanted to take you to. It's another centre where more detainees are taken."

"Please, please, Sir, let's continue," Helen said quickly. "I'll have to be alright. I want to find my fiancé today; if not, it may be too late."

"Okay then," the minister said. "Let's go."

They walked to his chauffeur-driven limousine and were driven to Kololo, one of Kampala's most affluent residential areas. They stopped at a seemingly private home, and the minister led her to a heavily fortified metal side door. An armed security guard opened the door for them, and as was in the previous detention room, a pungent stench engulfed them as soon as they stepped inside. The room was very crowded, with people crouching all over the place. Some of the people were limply sitting on the dirty benches, others crouching against the walls, and others were lying motionlessly on the floor. Most of the people were covered in blood, and many had gunshot wounds on their bodies. Cries and groans were heard from every side of the room.

The Minister took Helen first to the people on the benches against the walls, and staring at their faces in turn, he kept asking her if any of them was her fiancé. Again, her answer was "No" all along. He then held her hand and walked her through the crowd of people lying on the floor, and from time to time, he pulled their heads to show their faces to Helen, asking her if she recognised any of them. She didn't recognise any of them.

One man on the floor, with deep wounds on his arms and legs, raised his hand, slowly and in agony, towards Helen and crawled towards her. He grabbed her foot, and feebly said: "Please, madam, help me to get out of here. Honestly, I didn't do anything wrong; I was arrested by the GSU and was brought here. I don't know at all what for. I miss my wife and children terribly! Help me, please, please!"

The minster kicked the man's hands away from Helen's foot and sternly said to him: "Get off her immediately. The young lady can't help you. You'll just get yourself into deep trouble."

He pulled Helen aside and said to her: "Don't mind him or any of them. They're always annoying, and they can be very rough. Don't pay attention to any of them. Let's just move on." And so, they did, with Helen walking behind the Minister.

When they got about halfway down the room, the minister turned to Helen and asked: "How're you feeling? Do you still want to continue looking through this crowd, or do you want us to stop? If you do want to continue, I would suggest you continue looking by yourself, and you can take as much time as you wish. I'll be waiting for you by the exit door. If by any chance you find your fiancé, just give me a shout, and I will quickly get back to you and arrange his release. But you must be very careful, as some of these people can be quite violent and nasty."

Surprised, Helen looked at him and said: "That's all right, I'll continue looking on my own." She then took a deep breath and slowly walked on to continue looking through the crowds on her own. The stench in the room was as overwhelming as it was in the previous room.

She got to the end of the room, but, unfortunately, none of the people in the remaining crowd was Steven, her fiancé. So, she walked back to the minister and said: "None of them is my fiancé, sadly." And the minister said: "Can we then call it a day?" After a short pause, Helen reluctantly said to him: "Yes, we can stop for now, if you say so. But can we continue the search somewhere else soon, please? I don't mind doing so tomorrow."

"I'll see what I can do'" said the Minister.

As they were being driven away, the Minister said to Helen: "There are a few other places I could take you to, but as it's now quite late, it won't be possible tonight, but we can continue the visits tomorrow as you've suggested. I can arrange that and then let you know."

Helen, now close to tears, answered: "That'll be okay with me. But I fear tomorrow may be too late to find my Steven alive, don't you think so?" The minister didn't say anything, and they continued the journey in silence. When they got back to the Command Post, the minister quickly got out of the car, walked quickly to Helen's side, opened the car door for her, and said: "See you again tomorrow, possibly." She slowly got out of the car, and quietly thanked the minister.

As Helen walked towards her car, she heard somebody calling her name, from a distance. She turned towards where the call was coming from, and in a distance away, she saw a figure running towards her. She soon realised that it was Martin Oboo, her friend and work colleague at UPH.

"What the hell are you doing at Command Post at this late hour?" Martin asked her. "I'm very surprised to see you here!" Helen pulled him aside and almost in a whisper told him about Steven's disappearance. She then burst into tears.

"Steven, your fiancé?" Martin asked in astonishment. "Really? Why on earth should that happen to Steven? He's the last person I would expect to be taken away! Very upsetting news!"

He then added, "I can't forget the wonderful engagement party you and Steven thew for us on the boat; it's still very vivid in my mind! It was a party of all parties and one which all of us who attended will never forget!" He put his arms around Helen, pulled out his handkerchief and tenderly wiped away her tears. He then said: "I'll tell you what, leave it with me for now, Helen; I'll see what

I can find out from my uncle. I'm going to have dinner with him tonight, and whilst there, I'll have a quiet word with him to try and find out what information he has gathered since you went to see him. I doubt very much he ordered Steven's arrest. I'll see what I can get from my uncle and then get back to you as soon as I get any information. It is very shocking news! For now, however, please be strong for all of us – me, all your family and friends, and all your work colleagues at UPH. Okay, my dear?"

"I'll try my best to hold on, Martin," Helen said. "I can hardly wait to hear what information you'll get for me after speaking to the President. I'll be waiting eagerly and anxiously!" She gave him a peck on the cheek and quickly got into her car. She waved goodbye to Martin and drove off.

CHAPTER 3

LEAVE OR STAY IN UGANDA

Helen stayed at her home all weekend anxiously waiting for Martin Oboo's contact regarding what information he had gathered from the President on Steven's disappearance. She waited all Saturday and Sunday but received no contact from Martin.

'I wonder what the problem is,' she thought. 'Hasn't the President given Martin any information about Steven's disappearance? Does this mean that the President truly doesn't know anything about this? And can anybody believe him? I think it is now too late to find Steven alive.' Helen was now getting despondent.

Early on the morning of Monday, Martin knocked loudly on Helen's apartment door, and Helen opened it quickly. "Yes?" she anxiously asked him. "What's the news?"

Martin quickly locked the door behind him securely, led her to the lounge and asked her to sit down beside him.

"I'm sorry the news I've got for you is not good," Martin said, looking directly into Helen's eyes and squeezing both her hands. "I'm going to tell you everything I've managed to find out, and then you and I must decide immediately what you should do next."

"Tell me quickly, Martin, I can't wait! Please!" Helen shouted.

"Okay, okay. I'll tell you now. Please listen carefully," Martin said, with his hands now shaking.

He continued: "Over the weekend, I had conversations with the President, and this is what he told me. After you and Henry Kwach left the Command Post on Friday afternoon, the President wanted to see if he himself could get information about Steven's disappearance. So, he asked an officer from his office to gather information on what happened that Friday afternoon and report the findings to him as soon as possible. The officer carried out the investigation immediately, and by Saturday evening, the officer had submitted his findings to the President. The President shared with me some of the information. To say the least, I found the information quite upsetting. But all the same, I'll relate it to you, my dear.

"Apparently, Steven was arrested in error, regrettably: it wasn't him that the President wanted to be interrogated. He instructed the GSU to interrogate several senior lawyers and senior medical doctors whom the President believed were planning to overthrow his government, and Steven's boss, John Mende, was one of them.

"On that fateful Friday, three GSU soldiers were sent to the Ministry of Legal Affairs, where John Mende and Steven worked, to arrest John Mende and take him for questioning. Unfortunately for Steven, John Mende was out of the office when the GSU soldiers arrived. As the soldiers didn't know what John Mende looked like, they picked up whoever they found in his office. Unfortunately, this happened to be Steven. He was alone in the office he shared with John Mende. The soldiers roughly grabbed him and dragged him out of the office, pulled him along the corridor and finally out of the office building. At this time, Steven was struggling to be let free, and he was loudly asking the soldiers why they were arresting him, but none of them answered him. When the soldiers, with Steven, reached the army vehicle, Steven managed to look back at his office building, and he noticed that some of his work colleagues were standing on the office balconies and seemed to be surprised and shocked. He could hear loud cries from some of them.

"Apparently, Steven was heard pleading with his work colleagues: 'Please don't let them take me away. Please tell them that this is a mistake; I haven't done anything wrong!'

"Shut up, you fool," one of the soldiers shouted at Steven, and with great force, pushed him against the side of the vehicle, and his head hit it hard, causing a big cut on his forehead, and blood could be seen gushing out of it. One of the soldiers picked him up roughly and threw him into the back of the vehicle. 'You better keep quiet; otherwise, you'll regret your actions!' That soldier climbed into the back of the vehicle where Steven was lying on the floor. The remaining two soldiers jumped into the front of the vehicle, and they drove off speedily.

For some time, Steven's workmates stood motionless outside their offices, some of them with their hands over their faces, wailing helplessly.

The soldier in the back of the vehicle with Steven pulled Steven's head up and asked: "What's your name, you bastard?" Steven didn't answer, and the soldier repeated the question. Still, Steven didn't answer. The soldier slapped Steven across the face, but still there was no reaction from Steven. The soldier let go of Steven's head. It fell back on the floor, motionlessly.

"I think this man is a goner," the soldier in the back of the vehicle shouted to his colleagues in the front of the vehicle. "What are we going to do?"

"What?" the soldier driving the vehicle shouted, screeching the vehicle to a sudden stop. "You must be joking! What are we going to say to the Big Man? That we killed John Mende before he was interrogated. That'll be ridiculous!"

The soldier got out of the car and walked round to the back of the vehicle, jumped in, and pressed his ear against Steven's chest. "Yes, true, he's dead," he announced. "In this case, we better take the body straight to the mortuary." He got back in the driving seat and drove the vehicle in the direction of the nearest mortuary.

"I'm afraid, Helen, that from what we know so far, Steven was killed last Friday," said Martin sorrowfully. "I'm very sorry indeed to be the one to give you such devastating news!"

◆══════◆

Helen had her head in her lap all the time and was sobbing continuously. "I don't know what I'm going to do now," she muttered. "My life is over now. How'll I carry on without Steven in my life?"

"There is more, my dear," continued Martin, his voice grave and eyes clouded with worry. "But before I continue, let's first have a cup of tea. I'll go and make it."

He rose from the sofa, the weight of unspoken words palpable in the air. As Martin busied himself in the kitchen, the sound of the kettle whistling filled the room, a sharp contrast to the heavy silence that had descended.

Helen sat motionless, her mind a whirlwind of anxiety and dread. She clasped her hands tightly in her lap, her knuckles going dark from the strain. The ticking of the clock seemed louder, each second stretching into eternity. She tried to steady her breathing, but each inhale felt shallow, her chest constricted by an invisible vice.

Martin returned with a tray, the steam from the teacups rising like ethereal wisps, mingling with the tension in the room. He placed the tray gently on the coffee table and handed Helen a cup, his eyes searching hers for a glimmer of reassurance. She took the cup with trembling hands, the warmth seeping into her fingers, offering a momentary respite from the cold fear gripping her heart.

After a few sips of the tea, Martin sat back on the sofa, the creaks of the springs under him reminding him of the gravity of the moment. "There are urgent decisions to be made today, Helen," he said softly, his voice betraying the magnitude of the situation.

With her composure shattered, Helen bowed her head, tears streaming down her cheeks uncontrollably. Her sobs were raw, each wrenching from the depth of her being, echoing the profound anguish she felt. Her shoulders shook as she covered her face with her hands, the hot tears slipping through her fingers. The weight of Martin's words pressed heavily upon her, a tangible force that crushed her spirit. She could not find the energy to say anything more.

While they drank the tea, Martin continued with the story: "The President conveyed his sympathy over your fiancé's death, an innocent man, wrongly arrested and stupidly killed. I could see deep sadness in his eyes, and this is so unlike my uncle, the hard man he always displays. He said he could understand why you went directly to him, especially as your wedding was just a few weeks away. In silence, he paced up and down the room, I think, to sort out his thoughts.

"When he came to sit down again, his behaviour had completely changed. In a very loud voice, he said that when he asked Henry Kwach to assist with the search for your fiancé, and to get more information about you, he never expected him to take you to the detention centres. He always wanted these places to be restricted areas where no member of the public should go into without his permission, and that even Henry Kwach was aware of this condition. He said that if Henry Kwach wanted to get information for you from these centres, he should have gone into them by himself, collected the information for you, and then passed it to you. He should never, never have taken you there!" He then angrily said: "Henry Kwach was going to pay a big price for this mishap."

Martin continued: "Eventually, the President said that he was unhappy and uneasy about what you witnessed in those centres. Henry Kwach should never have let you see what goes on in those centres. After going into deep thought, the President said: 'I'm unsure and very worried that this girl,

Helen Mwanga, would be able to keep what she saw to herself. I'm certain she won't help herself from telling her family and friends about it, and word will go around the country and create havoc. She's, indeed, a nuisance to me! I must, therefore, decide quickly what to do with this Helen Mwanga, your work colleague."

Relating what the President had said about Helen, was making Martin agitated and he was extremely nervous indeed. He got off the sofa, went to the open window, and looked out anxiously; he remained quiet for some time, and when he turned around, Helen noticed that he was also crying. With tears running down his cheeks, he slowly walked back to the sofa, sat down close to her, and said: "And do you know, my dear? When my uncle says things like 'I must, therefore, decide quickly what to do with this Helen Mwanga, your work colleague.' I always know that he intends to get rid of the person concerned! This, therefore, makes me very worried and concerned about your safety!" He pulled Helen close to him, and they both cried. He then continued: "So, with a very heavy heart, I'm recommending that you leave the country as quickly as possible."

She quickly pulled away from him, walked to the window and blankly looked at the people walking on the street. 'I'll probably not be able to walk freely along the streets as those people are doing,' she thought. 'I'm sure if I don't leave the country I'll be killed within a day. So, should I leave, or should I stay? With my darling Steve dead, what will staying around mean to me? Permanent misery!'

Amidst lots of tears, she turned to Martin and said: "Leave the country as soon as possible? How can that be possible? I haven't made any travel arrangements; I haven't got even an air ticket. How can I possibly leave the country?" Martin took her hand and squeezed it. He steadfastly looked into her eyes, and said: "Don't worry, my dear, I'll go now and get your air ticket via the travel agency on the ground floor of this building; I know the staff there very well. Once I get it, I'll bring it to you straight away. We must also get you out of this flat as soon as possible. I know for sure that the army will be ordered to arrest you, and I bet they will find out where you live sooner than later!"

Helen stared at Martin blankly and said: "I'm most grateful that you got this information from the President for me, and your concern about my safety.

However, if he said that he didn't order Steven's death, wouldn't it be more appropriate for me to go back to him, and request him to get the culprits of this cruel act and have them charged for it? Why should I be the one to be punished? Why should I be forced to leave my beloved country? It's so unfair, Martin!"

"You really don't know my uncle," Martin said. If he thinks you can betray him, he will make you disappear without a trace. That's the truth. My advice to you is to leave the country sooner than later."

"You know your uncle best," said Helen. "I must agree with you on this; I need to leave Uganda immediately.

"What would happen if I didn't have you to advise me and help me with everything? I must be very grateful for having you as a loyal friend! I thank you sincerely and I'll do whatever you suggest. I don't think I have much choice, do I, Martin?"

"I'm afraid not," answered Martin, walking towards the door. Helen followed him, grabbed his hand, and, with tears still running down her face, said: "I know you offer such invaluable help only to your very special friends, and I'm thankful that I'm one of them."

Martin gave her a peck on the cheek and said: "I'll go get your ticket now. Do get your passport ready, and only the passport; nothing else. We don't want anybody to suspect anything. I'll be back very soon to take you to the airport. Okay, dear?" He quickly exited the flat.

In less than an hour, Martin was back with the air ticket. "Do you have your passport ready?" he asked. "We must leave immediately." He pulled her close to him and gave her a kiss on the cheek. She was now shaking like a leaf. He looked directly into her sad eyes and continued: "I know this is very distressing, but as I heard what the President said about you, I know that the best thing for you is to get as far away from him as possible. I hope you understand."

Martin took Helen's hand and led her down the stairs located at the back of the building to his car. He looked around them to make sure that there were no army soldiers anywhere in the vicinity. Once inside the car, Martin handed Helen a head scarf: "You better tie this scarf over your head to make it hard for anyone to recognise you easily."

"Thanks, Martin," Helen said as she took the scarf and tied it around her head. Martin started the car and began the journey to Entebbe airport.

The car was stopped for inspection by army soldiers at checkpoints situated along the road to the airport. However, as soon as the soldiers saw that it was Martin Oboo, the President's nephew, who was driving, they allowed the car to pass, and the journey to the airport went smoothly.

When they arrived at the airport, Martin stopped the car just outside the Departure entrance and quickly jumped out to open the car door for Helen. He held out his hand for her, gently pulled her out, gave her a tight but comforting hug, and said to her quietly: "Good luck, my dear friend. You'll phone me as soon as you get to Nairobi, won't you? I'd want to know that all went well. Come on, move on!"

"I'll, indeed, phone you as soon as I get a chance when I get to Nairobi, Martin," she said. "Once again, thank you very much for all the help you've given me. I can't thank you enough for all you've done for me. You're, indeed, a loyal friend! When you get back to Kampala, will you please do me a big favour? Will you please let my parents know what's happened to me? They'd be extremely distressed if they're not the first ones to learn about my flight from Uganda."

"Of course, I will!" answered Martin as he slowly let her go.

She quickly walked towards the Departure entrance. Just before she entered, she turned back and sadly looked at Martin and weakly waved to him and blew him a goodbye kiss. Martin waved back, almost in tears. She then entered the airport, thinking to herself: 'I hope I'll be able to get away without any hassle. I never imagined I would ever leave Uganda which I've always thought to be the best country to live in in the world. I feel incredibly sad indeed that I'm now leaving it, possibly for good!'

She checked in for her flight to Nairobi and went round the lounge to look for somewhere to sit. She found an empty bench where she sat, and as already related, she was joined by two lovely and helpful Catholic Sisters at the bench, and she was happy to sit with them during the flight to Nairobi. After exiting the airport, the three of them went to a small, well-kept garden nearby and sat down on a wooden bench, and Helen started relating her story to the Sisters.

The Sisters attentively listened to Helen relating the gruesome story of the killing of her late fiancé, Steven. The more they heard, the more emotional they became. In silence, both Sisters cuddled Helen tightly for quite some time. It seemed like forever! Sister Maria let her hands free, moved a little distance away. She looked into Helen's wet eyes intently and she said: "Helen, what an amazing and unbelievable story! Can't comprehend what you've been through!" Then Sister Martha looked closely at Helen and asked: "What are you planning to do now? And have you any idea of where you're going now?" Helen could not answer; she was now sobbing heavily.

The two Sisters looked at each other in silence, and this went on for quite a while. Then Sister Maria said to Sister Martha: "I don't think Helen is now in a state to answer what you're asking her. I think what we can do is to take her with us to the Convent and explain everything to the Mother Superior. I'm sure she'll understand and will be very sympathetic to Helen's situation. I have no doubt that she will agree to let Helen stay at the Convent for some days while the next step of her journey is decided. What do you think, Sister Martha?"

"Definitely," answered Sister Martha immediately. "That will be the best thing to do. Let's go now." They both pulled Helen up, walked to the taxi rank, and all three got into one of the taxis, heading to Westlands, a lovely residential area, on the outskirts of Nairobi, where their Convent was.

Upon arrival at the Convent, the Sisters went straight to the Mother Superior's office, tightly holding Helen's hands.

Mother Superior Georgina was a tall and sturdy woman, and she looked fearful in her thick-framed spectacles. She hardly smiled. The Convent Sisters were sometimes weary of her strictness.

When the two Sisters and Helen entered her office, she quickly stood up and walked towards them, her eyes fixed on Helen. "Hello, Sisters," she said, moving closer to Helen. "Who do we have here?"

"This is Helen," sister Maria answered. "But Mother Superior, can we please sit down first, and then tell you, her story? It's a long one!"

"Please do sit down," said Mother Superior. "I'm very intrigued!"

They all sat down by Mother Superior's desk, and then Sister Maria said: "Mother Superior, this young lady is Helen Mwanga: you will not believe what she has been through over the last few days. I'll relate her story to you on her behalf the best way I can, as I know she will get very emotional again if she relates it herself." Sister Maria then related Helen's story, checking with Helen from time to time the accuracy of the facts.

Mother Superior was very moved by the story; without a word, she stared at Helen in amazement. Sister Maria then leaned forward to Mother Georgina's desk and asked: "Mother, will it therefore be possible for this poor girl to stay here at the Convent while she works out what she will do next?"

"Of course, Sister Maria," answered Mother Superior. "She is welcome to stay here. Let her have some rest first; she badly needs it after all she's been through. At some point, we'll need to discuss with her what she wants to do next, and we'll then see how we can help her." She then walked over to Helen, who was now crying a lot, with her hands over her face. Mother Superior pulled Helen's face towards her and said to her: "Don't be so worried, young lady. We'll look after you well here, and you'll be very safe here. We'll all work together to see what is best for you." She gave Helen a big hug. Looking directly into her eyes, she continued: "These Sisters will look after you well, and when you've had a rest, we'll have another talk. Okay?"

"Yes, Madam, thank you very much. You've all been very kind to me," answered Helen. Sisters Maria and Martha then led her out of Mother Superior's office and led her towards the Convent's sleeping quarters and showed her a room where she would be sleeping.

"I'll go and get some essential items Helen will need during her stay here," said Sister Martha to Sister Maria. "In the meantime, you can take Helen with you to your room, and I'll join you soon."

"That'll be fine," said Sister Maria. "we'll see you soon in my room."

"You can come with me to my room to freshen up if you so wish," Sister Maria said to Helen: "If you'd like, we ca go to the canteen for something to eat and discuss what you want to say to Mother

Superior when we see her again in a day or two. Does that sound good to you?

"I'll appreciate that very much," said Helen. "I can't thank all of you enough for your exceptional kindness."

Whilst at the canteen Helen said to Sister Maria: "Can I please ask you for a big favour?"

"Please do, my dear," answered Sister Maria. "I'm listening."

"Will it be possible for you to arrange for me a phone I can use to ring my parents, please? I also want to contact Martin, the gentleman who assisted me in fleeing Uganda.

"We'll ask Mother Georgina when we go to meet with her again," said Sister Maria. "I'm certain she'll let you use the phone in her office." She added.

"That'll be great, thanks a lot," said Helen.

The following day was a beautiful sunny day, and Helen thought it was a good day for her and Sister Maria to meet with Mother Superior again to talk about her next move.

"How's our lovely guest settling in Convent life?" asked Mother Superior.

"Very well, thank you, Mother Superior," replied Helen. "Everyone has been so kind and extremely helpful, and I mean everyone," she continued as she gently placed her hand on Sister Maria's shoulder.

"Before we start the meeting, Mother Superior," said Sister Maria, "can you please allow Helen to use your phone to ring her family in Uganda?"

"But of course!" Mother Superior answered without hesitation. "Helen please follow me, and I'll take you where you can make the call in private." She led Helen to the inner room and showed her the phone. She closed the door and went back to Sister Maria. "Has Helen said to you yet what she wants to do next?" she asked.

"No. Not yet, Mother," Sister Maria answered. "Last night, she went through a few options, which she said she wanted to discuss with you today before deciding which one to take. I think it's best we wait for her to finish the phone call to her family, to go through the options with us. Maybe she'll be able to decide what is best for her by the end of the meeting."

"That's fair," said Mother Superior. "Let's wait for her to finish her phone call."

"Hi Martin," said Helen when she got through to Martin Oboo in Uganda.

"Hello Helen!" answered Martin, excitedly. "So pleased you've called, and from Nairobi! I was getting very worried; I'm glad you got there safely! I've been praying hard for you."

"I've already briefed your parents on your situation, and obviously, they're overly concerned and worried about everything. They're eagerly waiting to hear from you to let them know how the trip went and how you're coping with everything on your own. Your father, however, would want you to proceed to the UK as soon as possible. He's eagerly waiting for your call so that he can discuss the details with you. Perhaps you can phone him soonest."

"Thanks, Martin. But I was already planning to phone him immediately after speaking to you," said Helen. "Good old Dad! I miss him and Mum so much already. But did the GSU try to get me? I'm eager to know."

"Yes, my dear. They tried," said Martin. "Some army soldiers went to your apartment the day after you had left. But they obviously bounced, as you had already left! Your Dad already has the details about this; I prefer you get this story from him as it is very much connected to his proposals for your trip to the UK."

"Thank you so much for everything, Martin," said Helen. "You're indeed an invaluable friend, but I better say bye to you now and phone Dad ASAP." She rang her dad straight away.

"Hello, Helen, darling!" said her father as soon as he picked up the phone. "Your work colleague, Martin, kindly came over and told your mum and me what unimaginable things you've been through over the last few days and, of course, the horrendous passing of your beloved Steven! It sounds like a horror film, and your Mum and I can't comprehend how you've managed to survive! We're extremely proud of you!"

He then, added, "But you know, darling? Mum and I want you to move out from Nairobi; it's so close and accessible that the President's men could reach you in no time. So, since Martin told us your story, I have been to the British High Commission a few times, begging them to expedite the decision on your application for the scholarship to undertake a postgraduate degree at the London School of Economics. They were very sympathetic to your case, and guess what? They've agreed to bring your application forward, and I'm delighted to tell you that everything is now in place for you to travel to London from Nairobi as soon as possible!"

"What?" Helen screamed into the phone. "I can travel to London immediately? I can't believe that!"

"It is true, my darling," continued her father. "All the information about your scholarship for further studies at the London School of Economics has been sent to the British High Commission in Nairobi. You therefore need to go there as soon as possible, and the staff there will tell you what you need to do for your trip to London. Mum can't wait to have a quick word with you to congratulate you, and here she is." He handed the phone to Helen's mother.

"Hello, darling," said her mother, in tears. "It's great news, my darling, about your scholarship! We can only continue praying for you, and I'm sure the next stage of your journey will be much smoother. I love you so much, darling, and I miss you terribly! God bless you." Her mother handed the phone back to her father.

"Okay, darling?" said her father. "As Mum has said, we'll pray harder for you, and please do let us know how everything goes, right?"

"Yes, Dad, I can't thank you and Mum enough," said Helen. "You're the best parents I know in the whole wide world! Of course, I'll keep you posted on my movements. Love you both very much! Bye for now." She finished the call and walked back to Mother Superior's office.

Mother Superior and Sister Maria were chatting away when Helen returned. They immediately stood up and looked at her. "You look brighter and more cheerful now than before the call, Helen. Any good news from home?" asked Mother Superior anxiously. "Sit down first, though, and make yourself comfortable."

"Well," answered Helen, with a faint smile on her face. "The news is better than good; it's excellent news! My father has held meetings with the British High Commission in Uganda to request them to expedite my application for a scholarship to pursue further studies in the UK, and he's been successful! My application has been approved! This means that I can now travel to the UK as soon as I want! All the information about my scholarship has been forwarded to the British High Commission in Nairobi. So, I just need to go there to get the application for the scholarship finalised, including the issuance of the air ticket!"

"That's wonderful news, my dear Helen!" shouted Sister Maria as she jumped up from her chair to get closer to Helen. She put her arms around her and gave her a huge hug. "What can I say? You must be immensely proud of your parents!"

"Indeed, I'm!" answered Helen, beaming.

Mother Superior got up and, smiling from ear to ear, said: "Let's kneel down and thank the Lord for this wonderful act!"

All three of them knelt for the prayer, which was led by Mother Superior. At the end of it, she said goodbye to Helen and Sister Maria, and she warmly wished Helen good luck in the next chapter of her journey. Sister Maria and Helen then walked hand in hand out of Mother Superior's office and went back to the sleeping quarters to discuss what

Helen needed to do in preparation for her forthcoming trip to London.

Overjoyed, Helen said to Sister Maria that she would like to leave for London within a week's time, if all plans for the journey were completed. After a little while, Sister Maria and Helen joined Sister Martha in the canteen to update her on Helen's incredible story.

The following day, Helen went to the British High Commission in Nairobi to find out what she needed to do for her scholarship to the London School of Economics to be finalised. The High Commission had already received all the information from the British High Commission in Kampala, and they were expecting her to come to the High Commission in Nairobi any time, to be told what she needed to do.

"Good morning, Miss Mwanga," said Miss Elsa Jones when she came to collect her from the reception room of the British High Commission I Nairobi. "I am Elsa Jones who is handling your case. Please come with me and we can then discuss it." Elsa Jones led Helen to the sofa at one end of her office. "Please sit down here and make yourself comfortable," she said. "I'll get you a cup of tea before we start our conversation,"

Miss Jones, smartly dressed in a navy-blue two-piece suit, with matching blue high-heeled shoes, said to Helen: "I'm very sorry about what you've been through during the last few days. I hope that our conversation will be a pleasant change to what you've experienced lately.

"Your father has met our colleagues in the British High Commission in Uganda and related to them what horrible episodes you'd experienced, which made you flee Uganda so suddenly. Our colleagues in Kampala agreed with your father that you need to get away from any environs of Uganda as quickly as possible, and as such, you need to leave Nairobi quickly. Your father submitted all the required paperwork connected to your scholarship application for postgraduate studies at the London School of Economics and all this information is now here with us. Part of the approved scholarship is your travel expenses to London and your initial cost of living expenses in London. I can arrange all this for you quite quickly. What I need from you now is the date you wish to travel on, so that I can arrange your airline ticket and your initial accommodation in London. Think about these while you have your tea, and then tell me afterwards."

"Thanks so much, Miss Jones," said Helen. "Definitely, I will think about everything quickly, and we will then speak about them in a few minutes' time. I cannot believe that all this good news is for me, considering what I've been through lately! I'm speechless!"

"Don't worry about anything now," said Elsa Jones. "We'll do our best to look after you." Then she added.

Elsa then left Helen alone in the office to give her time to think about the information she had given her.

Of course, Helen would like to leave for London as soon as possible in view of the danger of abduction by the GSU she was facing. She was aware that the GSU personnel have been looking for her in Uganda, and they would easily get hold of her in Nairobi. Therefore, she needed to get further away from Nairobi and, indeed, the whole of East Africa. London would be a very safe option for her. However, she would need a few days to clear her mind before embarking on the next chapter of her life. So, she thought hard about everything Elsa had said.

In a few minutes, Elsa returned and sat close to her on the sofa: "Ready to talk now?" she asked.

"Yes, I am," Helen said. "I will be able to travel in a few days from now. Whichever day you can organise the ticket for me will be suitable for me."

"Very good then," said Elsa. "Leave it to me for now, and please do check with me tomorrow afternoon; I hope I will have everything sorted out for you. Is that okay with you?"

"Yes, Elsa," Helen answered. "I will come back to you tomorrow afternoon. Can't wait!"

"I'll see you tomorrow then. Goodbye for now," Elsa said.

Helen got up and skipped out of Elsa's office with a big smile on her face.

When Helen returned to the British High Commission in Nairobi the following day, Elsa was eagerly waiting for her in her office. Helen couldn't hide her excitement, even before hearing anything.

"Here is your air-ticket to London," said Elsa, handing the envelope with the ticket to Helen.

◆══════◆

"You're scheduled to travel to London a week from Thursday." Helen could hardly believe it. She jumped from the sofa and, with a brief scream, performed a little dance, smiling ear to ear! She moved close to Elsa and without thinking, went down on her knees and extended a hand to her and said: "Thank you very much, Elsa!" she said, almost in a whisper. With tears now running down her cheeks, she continued: "I don't know what else to say now, but may the good Lord bless you and all the High Commission staff for helping me so much in my time of dire need!"

"No worries," said Elsa. "We all wish you better luck in the next part of your journey." She then handed Helen another envelope and said: "Don't forget this further information about your initial accommodation in London and your upkeep funds. The Kenya High Commission in London has also been sent all the information about your case. So, please contact them when you get to London."

Helen got up and walked backwards towards the door with a huge smile. She then blew a kiss to Elsa before turning around and exiting the office. She ran straight to the Convent canteen, where she had promised to meet Sisters Maria and Martha for an update on her journey.

"Guess what! I'll be departing Nairobi for London soon," Helen announced as the three of them walked towards an empty table. They were all were incredibly happy and excited.

"My dear father, God bless him, managed to speed up my application for a scholarship at the British High Commission in Uganda for a two-year postgraduate course at the London School of Economics. You won't believe it, but everything went through swimmingly! I'm now holding the air ticket I collected from the Kenya High Commission a little while ago!" Helen said.

"What wonderful news!" exclaimed Sister Maria as she ran to Helen to give her a big hug in celebration. "When do you leave?"

"A week on Thursday."

"God is great," said Sister Martha when she too walked round to hug Helen. "I'm sure everything will be good for you from now on. We'll continue praying for you, dear girl. We better have something to drink to celebrate this momentous news." And that's what they did!

NEW BEGINNINGS

Helen had mixed feelings on her flight to London: on the one hand, she was excited that she was going to be as far away as possible from President Amin's killing gang, and on the other, she was getting away from the life and friends she had known all her life. What was her new life going to be like? She was determined to be as positive as possible; the new life in London was going to be a lot better than the killing fields of Uganda. The journey was made quite comfortable by the very friendly cabin crew on the British Airways plane.

Elsa Jones at the British High Commission in Nairobi had spoken to them about Helen's situation, and requested them to look after her, which they did very well. Upon arrival at London Heathrow Airport, one of the cabin crew girls volunteered to walk out of the airport with her to show her where to get a taxi. This made the start of her journey to the new life quite reassuring. She couldn't thank the cabin crew enough.

The hostel that Elsa Jones recommended to her was close to the London School of Economics, which Helen would be attending. The check-in at the hostel was painless, and Helen felt comfortable and safe there straight away.

The hostel was a modern, well-maintained building with a welcoming atmosphere. The common areas were bright and spacious, featuring cozy seating areas where students could relax or study. The walls were adorned with colourful artwork and posters from various international cultural events, reflecting the diverse community within the hostel. Her room, though small, was clean and well-arranged: it had a comfortable bed, a desk, and ample storage space.

The London School of Economics itself was a magnificent blend of historic and contemporary architecture. The main buildings, with their grand facades and classic designs, exuded an air of tradition and academic excellence. In contrast, the newer buildings featured sleek, modern designs with large glass windows, allowing plenty of natural light to flood in. The campus was dotted with green spaces, providing tranquil spots for students to gather and relax between lectures.

Helen was very happy that she was able to walk to the London School of Economics (LSE) for her lectures and was extra pleased that there were students from all over the world. She felt at home straight away, and she was welcomed by many fellow students. Within a few days, she started looking forward to her daily walk to LSE. The route took her through bustling streets lined with charming cafés, bookstores, and small shops, which gave her a taste of the vibrant city life.

She was also enjoying her course and was doing well at it, as well as the frequent mock exams she and her fellow students were sitting. The lecture halls were equipped with the latest technology, making learning both engaging and interactive. She passed her first-year exams comfortably. Her life now was a lot more enjoyable and happier than the one she escaped from, in Uganda.

Helen became a happy girl, and she enjoyed the company of her fellow students. However, when she was alone in her room, she often felt melancholy about her late fiancé, Steven, as well as her family in Uganda. She wished some of them were with her in London to share the wonderful time she was having. She missed all of them and, of course, home terribly.

Quite often, Helen and a small group of her college mates made it a habit of going to a nearby pub at the end of the day to relax and have a drink, as well as exchanging college gossip. Helen loved these get-together sessions as they stopped her reminiscing about the good life she had had growing up in Uganda.

During her second and final year at LSE, Helen and her college mates went to the pub one Friday evening for their usual social outing. For some unknown reason, Helen decided to dress more smartly than usual: it was always casual jeans and tee shirts. That evening, she wore a smart frock, and she also had some smart make-up on. To this day, she doesn't know why she decided to dress up smartly on that day. She entered the pub with her group and went straight to their usual table at the opposite end of the bar. They all ordered their usual drinks, and they started enjoying the evening. They were chatting away, teasing each other, and laughing away merrily.

When it was Helen's turn to get the drinks for the group, she walked to the bar to order and collect them. At the table next to the bar, there was a group of smartly dressed young men conversing joyously. Helen noticed that one of the gentlemen in the group was staring at her, and he had been doing so all evening. When she was about to pick up the drinks tray, this gentleman got up quickly, walked towards her and said: "May I please carry the tray for you?"

"That'll be very kind of you," answered Helen whilst she smiled nervously and shyly looking at him. The gentleman smiled widely back at Helen and asked: "My name is Jonathan. What's yours, and where are you from, smart lady? Few people come to the pub dressed so smartly!"

Getting a little embarrassed, Helen answered cheekily: "My name is Helen, I'm a student at LSE, and to be honest, I don't think I'm dressed smartly but thank you very much!"

He then carried the tray and followed Helen to her table. He put it down gently and then asked the group: "May I please sit with you here for a while?"

"Thank you for carrying our drinks," answered Doug, one of Helen's mates in the group. "And yes, you're welcome to sit with us."

"Thank you," Jonathan said, and then sat next to Helen and introduced himself to the group: "My name is Jonathan," he said. "I'm pleased to meet you all." They all, in turn, introduced themselves to him, too.

"You don't seem to have a drink, Jonathan; I'll go and get you one. You stay here," said Doug.

Jonathan was incredibly happy to be sitting next to Helen, and he glanced fondly into her eyes from time to time. He said to the group: "This friend of yours, I mean Helen, is very beautiful, don't you think so?" He looked around the group for reassurance. "I noticed her immediately your group entered the pub, and my eyes went straight onto her. I still can't take them off her. I must say, she is the most beautiful girl I've ever seen!"

There were eight people in the group, and all of them said: "Yes" in unison.

Doug came back with Jonathan's drink and stood with it in front of him. He held it for a while, as Jonathan didn't notice him immediately. He was only looking at Helen's eyes. "A drink for you, Jonathan," Doug said in a slightly raised voice. "Will you please take it?"

"Oh! I'm very sorry," Jonathan said as he stood up quickly, smiling. "Thank you very much, I'll have the drink, of course. But surely you can't blame me for being distracted by this gorgeous lady!" He took the drink and raised the glass, saying: "Cheers to you all., and thank you very much for bringing the lovely Helen with you to the pub when I happened to be there as well."

Helen was feeling quite embarrassed by Jonathan's compliments. 'I can't believe what I'm hearing,' she said to herself quietly. She turned and looked at Jonathan and said: "It's very kind of you. Thanks a lot. I'm very flattered!"

Jonathan stayed with Helen's group the whole evening; he was eager to learn about his new-found friends, their backgrounds and what they did. Most importantly, he wanted to know more about Helen. He also offered to buy a round of drinks for the group.

When the pub called "last orders", Jonathan turned to Helen and said quietly: "Do you mind if I give you a ride home?" I hope your friends are okay with that."

After a short silence, Helen said, looking at Jonathan: "That'll be okay, but can my friend Sarah come with us? We're staying at the same hostel. Do you mind?"

◆═══◆

"I don't mind at all; Sarah is welcome to come with us," said Jonathan. "The more the merrier!" He led Helen and Sarah to his car, and the rest of the group also left the pub and went in different directions.

When they arrived at the hostel, Sarah got out of the car immediately, thanked Jonathan for the lift, and ran off into the hostel, leaving Helen and Jonathan in the car, probably to give them a private moment. For a while, Jonathan and Helen remained quiet, both staring ahead through the windscreen. Jonathan then turned to Helen and, with a broad smile, said: "Thank you very much for a lovely evening, Helen. I enjoyed every minute I spent with you and your joyful friends. What a wonderful bunch of friends you all are! It was a pleasure meeting you all, and I hope we will all get together again soon."

"Glad you enjoyed our crazy gang," Helen said. "I, too, was pleased to meet you, Jonathan. I can't believe you enjoyed my company that much. I can't understand why!"

"It's because you're such a wonderful, nice and pleasant person," Jonathan said. "You stood out from your group when you all entered the pub. I couldn't take my eyes off you! And when you went to the bar to get the drinks for your group, I couldn't believe my luck; I knew that I had to take a chance to speak to you there and then! A voice inside me was saying: 'Jonathan, you can't let this chance pass; you must go to this lovely lady and introduce yourself!' And that's exactly what I did, and as they say, 'the rest is history' I can't believe I'm now sitting in the car with lovely you! I hope you don't think that I'm crazy!"

"No, Jonathan. Not yet!" said Helen immediately. "But you, too, are a very nice person and very handsome too!"

She extended her hand to him, smiling broadly. Jonathan took it and kissed it lightly. "Thank you very much for being you," he said. "I would, indeed, like to meet you again soon so that we can get to know each other more. What do you think?"

"I'd definitely love that," Helen answered, lifting Jonathan's hand and giving it a gentle peck.

"Great!" said Jonathan quickly, and, without hesitation, he asked: "What are you doing tomorrow evening, about six o'clock?" I can pick you up from here, and we can then go somewhere for a meal and a long chat. How about that?"

◆━━━◆

"That'll be perfect with me, Jonathan," said Helen. "I look forward to that. Can I please say good night now?"

"Yes, I think so," said Jonathan as he jumped out of the car. He ran to Helen's side of the car and opened the door for her. With a big smile, Helen looked up at him and said: "Thank you, Jonathan, you're indeed a true gentleman!"

Still smiling, Helen quickly got out of the car and started walking away quickly towards the hostel entrance. She stopped at the door and briefly turned back to look at Jonathan, who was leaning against the car and looking at her fondly. She gave him a wave and blew him a kiss.

"What a lovely gentleman I've met!" she muttered to herself as she entered the hostel. She skipped towards her room, smiling very broadly.

The following day, Helen's lecture hours couldn't go fast enough; she was just thinking of spending time with the gorgeous man she had met the previous day. What was she going to wear, and what was she going to tell him about herself at their first proper meeting? She would not like to say too much about what she had been through in case it scared him off her. Or, being such a lovely person, he would not mind hearing her story straight away, however unusual? She decided that she would let the conversation take its own course.

Soon after college that evening, she rushed back to the hostel to get ready for the outing. She made sure that she was ready at least fifteen minutes before six o'clock and anxiously waited for Jonathan. She was a bit nervous. Jonathan arrived at exactly six o'clock. Upon arrival, he got out of the car and rushed to open the passenger door for Helen. Helen ran out of the hostel straight to Jonathan's car when they gave each other a kiss on the cheek. "Do get in, please," said Jonathan. "You again look very smart!"

"Thanks very much, Jonathan," Helen said as she got into the car. "I'm looking forward to the evening very much. Where are you taking me?"

"That's a secret!" answered Jonathan with a cheeky grin.

He drove her and parked the car at the entrance of a Japanese restaurant. "With your luck, we've even got a parking space reserved for us just outside the restaurant," joked Jonathan. "It's never happened to me!" He quickly walked round to Helen's side of the car, opened the door for her, took her hand, and led her into the restaurant.

The restaurant bar was an elegant space with sleek wooden accents and soft, ambient lighting that created a warm and inviting atmosphere. Behind the bar, shelves were lined with an impressive selection of drinks, including Japanese sake, and the walls were adorned with Japanese artwork, adding a touch of authenticity and charm.

As they were a bit early for the meal, Jonathan suggested that they go to the bar area for a drink. They sat by the window just opposite a lovely park. He went to order the drinks from the bar, leaving Helen to admire the park in the fading evening light. He quickly came back with the drinks and sat down very close to her. "Cheers to a lovely evening!" he said, handing Helen her drink.

"To us!" Helen responded, and they both sipped their drinks.

"We have some time before dinner," Jonathan said. "We can perhaps chat about ourselves if that's okay with you."

"Yes, we can, but mine is a very long story, I'm afraid," said Helen with a smile. "I hope you won't get very bored. How long do we have?"

"We have the whole evening," said Jonathan. "And I'm very keen to hear it. May I please?"

Helen looked down at her lap and was silent for a while. She cleared her throat and briefly told her story, starting with the brutal killing of her late fiancé Steven, and culminating in her escape from Uganda, through Nairobi, Kenya, and ending up in London. When she finished the story, Jonathan pulled her head up and he saw tears running down her cheeks. He quickly pulled out a handkerchief from his pocket and, pulling her close to him, wiped away the tears. Without a word, he gently pulled her head to his shoulder and softly stroked the back of her neck. After some minutes, he pulled her head up, looked directly into her eyes, and said quietly: "My dear, you now don't have to worry about anything; you are in the best and safest place you can possibly be in. The only way for you now is up and up! Do you hear me? You're in very safe hands, too." He gave her a small peck on the neck and continued: "Can I have a big smile from you now? We can then walk to our table and hopefully to a new beginning for you. I'm sure about that."

Helen straightened herself and looked up to Jonathan, giving him a wide and cheerful smile. After tidying up her hair and wiping away the remnants of her tears, she said to him: "I hope it is indeed a fresh start for me. Thank you very much for listening to me and giving me your support too. I'm now very ready for our dinner; let's go and enjoy it!"

They walked hand in hand to their reserved table at one side of the restaurant by the window and started to select their food from the carousel as it moved around. They both found it great fun and very enjoyable. For Helen, it was the first time she had had a lovely and relaxed time since the abduction of her fiancé, Steven Rugara, in Uganda. Jonathan's presence, care, empathy, and good sense of humour, greatly contributed to the most enjoyable occasion their first outing turned out to be. Was this indeed a fresh and happy start for Helen? They had to wait and see.

When they next met, it was Jonathan's time to tell Helen about himself. "My story is a bit boring compared to yours," Jonathan said. "I'm an only child, and I grew up in Kent, where my parents lived and are still living. I went to the University of Kent to study engineering, graduating three years ago with a BSc degree. After graduation, I was incredibly lucky to get my first, and still my current, job at the Ministry of Works in London. I was very pleased to be able to move to London, as I always wanted to move to London for a change of scene, as I had lived in Kent while growing up and studying, staying at home with my parents. I loved living with my parents, but I wanted to start life away from them and make a home on my own. I've made a lot of friends with my work colleagues, and I am currently sharing a flat in Kensington with one of them, Keith Brown. Keith is a lovely man, and we get on very well. I've no doubt that you'll like him when you meet him. If I hadn't moved to London, I'm very sure that I wouldn't have met special people like you!" He pulled Helen towards him and gave her a big kiss. "You're a very special lady, and I'm very proud to have met you!"

Helen and Jonathan enjoyed each other's company very much, and as Jonathan's places of work and Helen's university were close to each other, they often met for drinks or meals at the end of the working day. Jonathan was always happy to give her a lift back to the hostel. They both looked forward to these meetings very much.

Helen's college mates noted her change from a sad, introverted girl they saw when she started at LSE to a happy, smiley, and jovial girl. She, however, didn't want to elaborate to them about her relationship with Jonathan. She thought that by doing so, might be tempting fate! She didn't want to experience again the sad end of a relationship like it was with her relationship with Steven.

Jonathan wanted to give a surprise to Helen: he arranged a weekend away from London for them. "I'm sure you'd appreciate getting away from the hustle and bustle of London for a couple of days," he said to her over the phone. "Wouldn't you?"

"Of course, I'd love it, love it very much, Jonathan!" answered Helen.

"Okay, I'll collect you from the hostel this Friday evening," said Jonathan. "The destination is a surprise!" he added.

"Oh! Very interesting, I'll be anxiously waiting," said Helen.

When Jonathan arrived to collect her, Helen asked: "Where are you taking me this time?" as she fastened her safety belt in the car.

"It's again a secret!" answered Jonathan with a giggle, "but I'm sure you'll not be disappointed."

"Another secret!" remarked Helen. "You're giving me a few of these, but I'm glad to say that I haven't been so far disappointed with any of them!"

They arrived at their destination as the sun was going down. It was Brighton Beach, and it looked idyllic!

"This is it," said Jonathan after stopping the car.

"It looks beautiful," remarked Helen, "and I adore the seaside!"

After checking in at their beach hotel, Jonathan took Helen's hand and led her upstairs to their room; they unpacked and freshened up before going to the dining room for supper. They were to be looked after by a very pleasant waiter, who led them to their table, and he took their orders for drinks. He returned with the drinks and the menu leaflet for them to choose their dishes.

"It is great to get away from the busy life of London for a while. Thank you very much for organising this, Jonathan," said Helen. "Next time we go out of London, it'll be my turn to spoil you, although I might need your help in selecting the venue. No arguments, please, do you hear?"

Jonathan just gave her a naughty look and smile, and without saying a word, he looked down at his menu sheet. "Can we order our meals now?"

After their meal, Jonathan took Helen's hand and led her upstairs to their room. They sat on the bed, still holding hands. He looked into her eyes lovingly and moved closer to her, pulled her towards him, and gave her the first passionate kiss on the lips. Though Helen was very surprised, she didn't resist at all; they fell flat on the bed and continued kissing, and this seemed to go on forever! They eventually pulled apart, each had a quick wash and changed into their nightwear. They sat up in bed and chatted about all sorts of things before going under the duvet. Jonathan pulled her towards him and extended another loving kiss to her, which she, again, didn't resist. They held onto each other tightly, adoringly looking into each other's eyes, and they harmoniously made their first love, which they both enjoyed very much. Thereafter, they fell asleep.

The following morning, Jonathan woke up first and he didn't want to wake Helen up yet. He quietly ordered their breakfast to be brought up to their room, over the intercom. He laid it at the little table in the room and tiptoed back to the bed, sat down by Helen's side, bent down towards her, and with a gentle kiss, he whispered: "Breakfast is ready, darling."

She slowly opened her eyes, slowly sat up, and, with a loving smile, said: "Thanks, darling; I'm so ready for it." She put her arms around him and gave him a big kiss on the lips. They got off the bed and walked to the breakfast table. "I'll be mother," she said as she started plating the breakfast food. They lovingly shared a nice breakfast.

After breakfast, Jonathan suggested they take a walk along the beach, as the weather was wonderfully warm. They strolled hand in hand, the morning tranquility enveloping them. The beach, still quiet and almost empty, rightly offered a serene escape from the hustle and bustle of London. Finding a bench shaded by a tree, they sat down and gazed at the sea and the gentle waves providing a soothing backdrop.

After a while, Jonathan reached into his pocket and pulled out a small white box. With a tender smile, he took out a ring and knelt before Helen. "Helen, will you marry me?" he asked, his voice filled with emotion.

Helen, surprised and overwhelmed with joy, looked into his eyes, tears of happiness welling up. Smiling broadly, she threw her arms around his shoulders: "Of course, yes, Jonathan, my darling! I will marry you! Thank you for asking!"

Jonathan rose quickly, embracing her warmly and slipping the engagement ring onto her finger. They shared a long, lingering kiss, their hearts full of love and excitement. "We should head back to the hotel and celebrate this, darling!" Helen exclaimed, her joy making her dance with happiness.

"Yes darling, let's do that," said Jonathan, as he took her hand and led her back to the hotel. "But I think, for this momentous celebration, we should go to central Brighton for a special dinner. When we get back to the hotel, I'll ring around some places to find a nice restaurant and book a table for us. Surely, what my darling Helen has been through in the recent past, she deserves a wonderful dinner tonight, definitely!" They then engaged in a tight, loving embrace and then walked briskly back to the hotel.

Jonathan managed to find a nice and cozy restaurant in a very nice area of Brighton, which they drove to in the early evening. When Jonathan booked their dinner table, he casually mentioned that they had got engaged earlier that day, and the restaurant left no stone unturned to deliver to them the befitting dinner. The restaurant manager requested the other diners to join him and his staff in congratulating the happy couple while they cut the well-decorated cake the restaurant got for them. Helen was overwhelmed, and she shed happy tears in appreciation of this wonderful gesture by the restaurant. She was thinking: 'Yes, this is, indeed, a major turning point of the recent timorous chapter of my life!'

On their way back to the hotel, Helen was quiet and demure. "What's the matter?" Jonathan asked her. "Suddenly, you seem sad. I thought both of us should be extremely happy now that we have each other. I hope you're not changing your mind about our engagement!"

"No, no, no, darling! Don't ever think that!" said Helen. "I'm ecstatic about our engagement, but it's so sad that my family can't be nearby to share this great news with us. There'll also be no way for them to come over to the UK for our wedding. That's why I feel a bit sad. I'm very sorry, but I can't help thinking about it."

"I fully understand that, darling," said Jonathan, wrapping his arms around Helen and giving her a passionate kiss. "But don't worry, me, my mum and dad will always be there for you. You'll be the daughter my parents didn't have, and, I must say, their only daughter! I'll tell you what, when we get back to the hotel, we'll phone both sets of our parents and give them the good news! How about that?"

"Yes, darling, that'll be great," answered Helen. "And you'll be able then to ask my father for my hand in marriage."

"What will we do if he says no?" joked Jonathan.

"That'll never happen!" said Helen confidently. "He'll be the happiest man alive! Let's hurry up to make the calls. I'm now very excited!"

As soon as they got back to their hotel room, they made the call first to Helen's parents to give them the wonderful news. Helen spoke to her father first to tell him what was happening to her. She then passed the phone to Jonathan and said: "Go on then, introduce yourself to my dad, and then ask him the big question!"

"Good evening, Mr. Mwanga," Jonathan started the conversation. "My name is Jonathan Taylor. I've fallen head over heels in love with your gorgeous daughter, Helen. Will you please allow me to take her hand in marriage?"

"That's the best news I've heard regarding Helen in recent months!" answered Helen's father, excitedly. "My answer is YES, but I need to confirm that with Helen's mum seated here next to me." After a brief pause, he came back to the phone and announced: "YES! Both my wife and I fully grant you our permission to marry our daughter Helen. It is, however, so sad that we will not be able to attend the wedding. We request you to look after her well; she is incredibly special to us."

"I will, indeed, sir, she is very special to me, too," said Jonathan. He then handed the phone back to Helen, and performed a joyful dance around the room, loudly saying: "Yes, yes, yes, I've got your parents' permission to marry you!"

Next, they spoke to Jonathan's parents, who were equally very happy and excited about the engagement and forthcoming wedding.

Helen graduated from LSE with an MA degree, specialising in Human Resource Training and Development. Jonathan and his parents, William, and Susan Taylor attended her graduation ceremony. As it was Jonathan's parents' and Helen's first meeting, Jonathan took the opportunity to introduce them to each other. Jonathan's parents were happy to represent Helen's parents at the ceremony, and they were enormously proud of her achievement. When Helen was walking back to her seat with the degree roll in her hands, Jonathan and his mother walked quickly to her to congratulate her. Just before they got to her, Jonathan let his mother go ahead of him to shake her hand first. She extended her hand to Helen and said to her: "Congratulations to you! Very well done, my dear! We're all very proud of you."

"Thank you very much, Mrs. Taylor," replied Helen, smiling politely. "I'm very privileged that you all came to my graduation." But before she could say anything else, Susan Taylor grabbed Helen's arm, pulled her towards her and gave her a big hug. She looked straight into her eyes, and, with a big smile, said: "Helen, I am not Mrs. Taylor to you; I'm Mum to you! That's what I am, and will always be, to you! Do you hear that, my darling?"

"Yes, Mrs. Tay… sorry, Mum," replied Helen. "I'm deeply sorry I made that error again! I promise I will not do that again." She then moved and stood between Jonathan and his mother, pulled them both towards her and kissed each one on the cheek, and turning to Mum, said: "I'll always love you very much, my dear Mum!" The three of them then walked slowly towards Jonathan's Dad, who was now standing up and patiently waiting to give Helen a warm congratulatory embrace.

When the ceremony ended, Jonathan drove them to a London restaurant where they had a fabulous celebratory dinner.

A few weeks after Helen's post-graduation, Jonathan decided to move from his shared accommodation to his own place. He found a two-bedroom flat along Finchley Road in North London. Before he moved in, he took Helen to see it. Helen loved it and thought it would be very convenient for Jonathan: it was close to a shopping centre and was also very close to a tube station. When Jonathan saw how excited Helen was over it, he asked her if she would consider moving in with him.

"Of course, I'd love that," said Helen. "It would be nice to move from the hostel to a private place where total privacy would be almost guaranteed. Thanks a lot, Jon. When I also start to earn some pennies, we'll share the rent, won't we?"

"That'll be up to you, my darling," answered Jonathan. "I think I'll be moving into the new flat within one week, and you can join me any time after that."

Helen decided to let Jonathan settle well into the new place before she moved in, and after two weeks, she was ready to join him. Jonathan collected her from the hostel with the few personal effects she had and drove her to the new flat. "Come on in," he said, as he ran from the car to open the flat door for her. "Welcome home, my love!"

◆━━━◆

Helen followed Jonathan closely, ran to the bedroom, jumped onto the bed, and said: "Comfortable bed, and a good start for our life together!"

"Indeed, darling," said Jonathan as he, too, jumped onto the bed to give Helen a long, loving kiss.

After obtaining her postgraduate degree, Helen started looking for a job in her area of expertise. One Saturday morning, while she and Jonathan were still in bed, she casually flipped through the magazine that came with the weekend newspaper, and she noticed an interesting advert, which made her sit up immediately. She read it over a few times before turning to Jonathan, who still had his eyes closed: "Wake up, Jon and look at this advert. An international organisation based in London is looking for a person with a qualification in Human Resource and Development, which, as you know, is my field! Do you think I could be a candidate for it? Please look at the advert and let me know what you think."

Jonathan moved closer to look at the advertisement. They both read it in silence.

"I can't think of a more appropriate candidate for that job than you, darling!" exclaimed Jonathan. "I would urge you to apply without delay. What do you think?"

"Of course, I'll apply," said Helen. "Can you please help me with composing the application as soon as we've had breakfast? I would like to submit the application as soon as possible. Maybe I could get the job!"

"I'm thinking the same," said Jonathan. "We must start on the application ASAP, even before breakfast." They both jumped out of bed and went to the dining table, and Helen started drafting the application. She passed each page she wrote to Jonathan for comment. By lunchtime, the first draft was completed, but they decided to have a break from it until the following day, and they started getting the breakfast ready. They came back to it and got it ready for posting on Monday.

"I have a strong feeling that this is the job for you, darling," said Jonathan. "Please make sure you don't forget to post it first thing on Monday morning."

"I won't forget, darling," Helen responded. "It's very important to me."

Soon after breakfast on Monday morning, Helen took the application, pushed it into the letterbox very close to their flat, and she skipped back to the flat, whistling a jolly song. Thereafter, she and Jonathan just waited for a response from the advertiser, if at all.

◆━━━◆

A month after posting the application, a letter addressed to her arrived at the flat. It was 4.30 pm, and Helen was alone at home: Jonathan had not yet come back from work. She noticed that the sender was the international organisation she had applied to. She held the letter in her hand for some time, and she was shaking as she could not bring herself to open it: 'It could be a regret,' she thought. 'Or could be a positive response!' She walked slowly to the dining table and slowly sat down with the letter still unopened. She stared at it for a few seconds, took a deep breath, and with her heart pounding, she quickly opened the envelope, pulled out the letter, and started reading it.

"Wow, wow!" she shouted to herself as she jumped off the chair. "An invitation for an interview! I can't believe this! How can my luck change so much in such a short time?" Without realising it, she burst into tears, and knelt on the floor sobbing, with the tears falling on the letter she was still holding tightly in her hands.

Within a few minutes, she heard the key turning at the front door. Jonathan was back from work. When he came in and noticed that Helen was on the floor, he ran straight to her, asking: "What's the matter, darling? What has happened?" He, too, knelt beside her and wrapped his arms around her.

Without a word, Helen handed him the letter. He read it and immediately screamed and jumped up: "This is great news!" he exclaimed. "It's very hard to believe, but it's true! Get up, my darling; we need to start preparing you for the interview. You must get this job, no matter what happens!"

They both got up, and while hugging each other tightly, they walked to the dining table. "Sit down, my darling," said Jonathan, "and stay there. I'll make you a scrumptious meal to celebrate this unbelievable change in your luck!"

Helen went for the interview at the organisation's office in London. She had prepared well for it, but all the same, she was quite nervous as she sat in the waiting room just outside the interview room. When she entered the interview room, she saw that all the six members of the board were smiling, and this melted away her nervousness. She learnt later that, after studying her application, the interview panel had marked her as a very suitable candidate for the advertised job. So, they were pleased to see her at the interview. As the interview was relaxed, she enjoyed every bit of it.

The one-hour interview was over within a flash! At the end of it, all the board members smiled at her as they bade her goodbye.

Two weeks after the interview, Helen received a letter from the organisation offering her the position of Human Resource Officer in their Human Resources Department. She could hardly believe it. She accepted the appointment right away and informed them that she would be able to commence work in two weeks' time. Jonathan was very excited about, and extremely proud of, Helen's success in getting a job befitting her qualifications, and with one of the prestigious international organisations.

With her first salary, Helen shared the flat rent with Jonathan, as she had promised, and she carried on doing so month after month. She could not believe that in just over two years since escaping from Uganda, she was now able to make a home in London, UK, with a wonderful man, Jonathan, by her side! She looked up to the sky and thanked the Lord for the continuing blessings.

Their wedding took place soon after Helen started working. It was held at a small, cozy church near Jonathan's parents' home in Kent, and the reception was held in a nearby social hall, and both functions were attended by Jonathan's family as well as many of his and Helen's workmates, friends, and acquaintances. All the attendees thoroughly enjoyed the occasion.

Unfortunately, none of Helen's family were able to come to the wedding due to the continuing instability in Uganda. Helen felt a deep sadness, a pang of loneliness amidst the joyous preparations, knowing her loved ones would not be there to share this special moment with her. However, her spirits were lifted when her parents managed to send a congratulatory telegram to the couple. As it was read out at the reception, Helen's eyes filled with tears, and a warm smile spread across her face. The heartfelt message brought a sense of closeness to her family despite the distance, and that, indeed, made Helen's day.

CHAPTER 4

DEVASTATING NEWS FROM UGANDA

Helen and Jonathan tried to take it easy at the weekends as they were both terribly busy at their work. They enjoyed having a lying-in in bed on Saturday and Sunday mornings. Very often Jonathan woke up before Helen and sneaked out to make breakfast for them, which they usually had in bed. One Saturday morning, a phone call came from Helen's mother, and Helen answered it.

"Darling, you won't believe this," Helen's mother said, her voice trembling. "Your brother Denis was killed last night. We have only just been told!"

Helen's heart sank, and she gripped the phone tighter. "How and why?" Helen screamed, her voice breaking. "You are right, Mum, I cannot believe it! We lost Steven not so long ago, and now Denis!

What happened?" Her mind swirled with shock and disbelief, unable to grasp the cruel reality.

"Apparently, Denis was alone in his lounge reading, after his wife and kids had gone to bed. He heard a knock on the door and opened the door. There were three soldiers, obviously from the GSU, standing there holding guns."

"May I help you, gentlemen?" Denis asked.

"You're a doctor, aren't you?" asked one of the soldiers. "All of you, stupid doctors, are conniving to overthrow the Government! But you will not succeed! You will all be gone before you do so!"

"Before Denis could answer," Helen's Mum continued, "one of the soldiers pointed his gun at him and shot him in the chest, obviously killing him. He fell forward and never got up. And that was the end of our poor Denis! His poor wife didn't realise what had happened to her husband until early morning the next day. When she woke up and did not see him in bed, she assumed he was downstairs making a cup of tea. She went downstairs to join him but noticed that the front door was ajar. She walked to it and immediately saw the horror in front of her! Her dead husband!

She went down on her knees beside him to try to resuscitate him, but he was dead, and very cold!"

"Oh, Mum, that's awful!" Helen said, with tears running down her face. "Why Denis? It is so unfair!"

"I suppose because he was a medical doctor. As you know, the doctors and the lawyers are being butchered left, right and centre!" answered Mum.

"When will this brutality end, Mum?" Helen screamed into the phone, with streams of tears running down her cheeks!

Jonathan, who was in the kitchen getting breakfast ready, heard Helen's screams, and he ran to the bedroom: "What's the matter, darling?" he asked as he sat next to her on the bed. "Who's on the phone?"

"It's Mum," answered Helen, with a trembling voice, "with more shocking news! My eldest brother Denis was murdered last night by Idi Amin's gang!"

Jonathan took the phone from her: "Hello Mum, I'm so sorry to learn of Denis' passing," he said to Helen's mother. "Please accept our deep condolences for the sad loss. We're both with you,

Dad, and the rest of the family, in spirit and mind. If there is anything we can do to help from here, please do let us know."

"Thanks, Jonathan," said Mum, her voice clearly strained from excessive crying. "There is not much you can do, only to pray for Dad and me. Dad is beside himself with sorrow and anger. That is why it is me ringing you, instead of him. He is in pieces!"

"Both Helen and I are very sorry indeed," Jonathan said, "and we sympathise with you all." He then handed the phone back to Helen.

"Mum, we're both devastated," said Helen. "It's a pity that we can't be there with you, Dad, and the family, to share the sadness, and to help in any way. Please do keep us posted on the funeral arrangements. And please pass our condolences and love to Dad, Denis's wife, his kids, and all the family. We both love you very much and miss you terribly. Thank you very much for phoning us. God bless you, Mum! Bye for now."

"It's very sad that Amin is continuing to persecute the medical doctors, just because he had a disagreement with one doctor in the past," said Helen as she took her breakfast tray from Jonathan.

"What will happen to Uganda after he's killed off all the doctors? I feel very sorry for my country."

"So do I," said Jonathan as he sat down beside her to have breakfast with her.

Much as Jonathan had done for Helen up to now, to try and distract her from her previous sad events, the killing of her eldest brother, Denis, upset her a great deal, and Jonathan was getting very concerned about her. However, he did not give up: he continued coming up with all sorts of activities to cheer her up. So, for her first annual leave from work, he proposed taking her to the USA for a short holiday. He knew it would be a great joy for her as he was aware that Helen always wanted to visit North America, particularly New York and Los Angeles. He booked a two-week holiday to New York and Los Angeles. This cheered Helen to no end, and she could hardly sleep for two days before their flight to New York.

Although it was a long flight, they both did not worry about it, as they were looking forward to touring some parts of the USA for the first time. They stayed at the lovely Park Lane Hotel, close to Central Park, and the hotel was near the places they wanted to visit – the galleries, museums, and, of course, the shops. They thoroughly enjoyed each day's activities.

On their last evening in New York, Helen wanted to express her thanks to Jonathan for arranging the holiday, by taking him to a film show in New York, and to dinner afterwards. She took him to see the 'Flash Dance' film, which was playing in cinemas in New York. They both enjoyed it immensely. Thereafter, she took him to dinner at a nice Mexican restaurant in downtown New York.

The following day they flew to Los Angeles, principally to go to Disneyland. They both always wanted to visit Disneyland, and they both became kids again, thoroughly enjoying participating in many of the Disney activities.

They also had the opportunity to go around amazing shopping centres, and they were also taken to view the impressive mansions of the very rich, from a distance. After a week in Los Angeles, they flew back to London. They were exhausted and jetlagged, but they, for sure, had had a wonderful holiday.

"Where will I be without you, Jon?" Helen said, with a big smile on her face, and as she stepped into a warm, soapy bath, Jonathan ran for her.

"Me either!" retorted Jonathan as he joined her in the inviting, soapy bath.

As both Helen and Jonathan had good jobs, and both received good salaries, they decided to buy a two-bedroom house in Hampstead, a nice residential area of London. They were able to pay for the mortgage comfortably between them. A few months after moving into their new home, Helen became pregnant, and she and Jonathan were very excited and overjoyed with the prospect of becoming parents for the first time. During the next few days, they could only think and talk about their forthcoming bundle of joy: the baby's sex, its weight, the names they would choose for him/her, etc. The following weekend, they went over to Kent to give Jonathan's parents the wonderful news. They also couldn't wait to phone Helen's parents to let them know, too. The two sets of parents were extremely excited about becoming grandparents.

A few days after Helen's parents had received the news of Helen's pregnancy, a phone call came from Helen's mother. Helen and Jonathan assumed that she just wanted to have a chat with her daughter to advise her on what to do, and not what to do, during the pregnancy. It was Jonathan who picked up the phone: "Hello, Mum. How are you?" he said, cheerfully.

"Not very well, Jonathan," she replied. "I haven't got good news at all, and I need to speak to Helen urgently. Can you please put her on the line?"

"Helen, it's your Mum," Jonathan said. "She wants to have a word with you urgently. Please come quickly."

Helen ran from the bedroom and took the phone: "Hi, Mum, what's the matter now?" she said. Her mother couldn't say anything right away; she was weeping softly.

"Mum, what's the matter?" Helen asked. "Please tell me!"

"More bad news, I'm afraid, my dear," her Mum said. "I'm sorry to be giving you bad news whenever I phone, but I must tell you. Your second brother, Philip, has also been killed! No doubt, on Amin's orders!"

"What?" Helen screamed into the phone. "Two brothers killed within a few weeks of each other! This is unbelievable! So now I have no brother left!" She cried loudly. "How, where, and when did this happen, Mum?"

"My dear, your second brother, too, met a gruesome death!" Mum said. "As you know, Philip had been posted to Tororo Hospital in Eastern Uganda, to take charge of the team of doctors there. He'd been there for just one year, and the doctors at that hospital loved him very much. They said he was a superb doctor and a supportive boss. As a way of motivating the team further, Philip organised a party for them at the weekend at his house. He provided plenty of food and lively music for them. They were having a good time, and many of them couldn't stop themselves from getting on the floor to dance. The music was blaring away when three soldiers carrying guns on their shoulders entered the room. They went straight to the food table, happily chatting away between themselves, and they started serving themselves. The guests were very shocked to see them, and they slowly moved away, and just looked on from a distance. Philip went over to them and asked: "Who're you? I didn't invite you to the party, did I?" The three soldiers turned round at the same time to stare at him but did not answer his questions. He then continued: "Can you please leave? You're carrying guns, and my guests are very scared of them."

"One of the soldiers moved very close to Philip and looked directly into his eyes and said: 'We don't have to be invited, do we? We go wherever we want. You are a doctor, with loads of money. Answer me!" He grabbed both Philip's hands, and, still staring at him, continued: "You and other doctors and lawyers are planning to overthrow the government! But you will not now!" He quickly pulled a machete from under his jacket and, in one go, forcefully slashed the side of Philip's neck, almost severing his head off! Blood immediately gushed out of his neck, as he fell onto the floor, with a thump! On seeing this, many of the guests screamed, and some of them ran towards Philip, to try and do something to save him. With a nasty grin, the soldier looked around the room and then walked towards the door, followed by his two accomplices, and went outside. They got into their vehicle and drove away fast.

"The guests were totally stunned, and many of them were now crying. One of the guests ran to the phone and called the ambulance. Upon arrival, the ambulance team examined Philip, and pronounced him dead, unfortunately. His wife, Susan, and his two young children were also in the room and witnessed what happened. Susan fainted and fell to the floor. She was carried away and taken to the ambulance by the ambulance personnel and was taken to hospital, together with her dead husband.

So, darling Helen, sadly, we'll be burying Philip so soon after Denis.

"To make matters worse, the news of Philip's death affected your dad very badly: he too collapsed with a suspected heart attack; he is now in hospital undergoing tests, and he has not said a word since we received news of Philip's killing. I am extremely worried about him." Mum was now crying uncontrollably, and she hung up the phone at that point.

Jonathan was standing close to Helen and had his arms around her. Before he could ask her what the bad news was about, she suddenly slipped from his hold and fell to the floor and, she too, fainted!

"Helen, please don't do this to me," shouted Jonathan. "I love you and the baby so much. I don't want to lose either of you!" He picked her up, carried her to the bedroom, and laid her on the bed. He then rang NHS and told them about her, and an ambulance was sent immediately to take her to hospital, and Jonathan went with her. At the hospital, Jonathan was told that Helen would be kept in the hospital until the medical staff were sure that she and the unborn baby were fine. He could, therefore, go home for some rest. So, he went home to phone their parents to let them know what had happened to Helen.

When Helen woke up later, she immediately requested to be allowed to go home, but the hospital staff explained to her that they would discharge her after they were certain she and the baby were out of danger, and she agreed to that. In the meantime, she would be monitored closely and continuously by the staff.

Two days after arriving at the hospital, Helen started getting stomach pains, and these were followed by bleeding. The bleeding gradually became heavy. The hospital staff did everything they could for Helen, but despite all their efforts, Helen sadly lost the baby. She was, of course, devastated, and when Jonathan returned to the hospital later and was told about it, he, too, was very upset. He hugged his wife to comfort her, and, lovingly, said to her: "I know we're both extremely sad about the loss of our baby, but I don't want you to take it too badly; I'm sure we'll be able to expect another child soon, and we will have more children, if we so want, thereafter. As of now, my darling, my main concern is to get you better as quickly as possible, so that I can take you home soon. That's the best for us." Within a few days after, Helen was discharged and was allowed to go home.

Before Jonathan returned to the hospital, he phoned Helen's mother in Uganda to tell her about what had happened to Helen, and the sad loss of their unborn baby. He told her that this happened soon after Mum phoned to tell Helen about the death of her second brother, Philip. Mum said she was very sad about losing the grandchild who she and Dad were so much looking forward to getting. She blamed herself for causing the miscarriage by phoning them to give them the devastating news. She, however, said she would give Dad all their news when he is fully conscious, but she said that she was so sure that this news would delay his recovery. Before saying goodbye, she conveyed her and Dad's condolences on the sad loss of the baby.

The following day, Helen's mother telephoned Helen and Jonathan, again with more bad and, sad news: Helen's father had passed away! He had sadly passed away peacefully in his sleep the previous night. She told them that when he came round briefly, he had requested her to ask them to promise that they would travel to Uganda as soon as peace returned to the country, possibly through a change of government. He desperately wanted to meet his son-in-law, Jonathan, face to face, as he longed to give him a big hug; he had said that he had wanted to do this for a long time.

"Now that your loving Dad has gone," Mum said, "I'm hoping that you will be able to come to Uganda sooner rather than later, so that I can give you both huge hugs on his behalf. I'm sure he will be looking down on us when this happens, with a big smile on his face!"

"We would love to come over," Helen said to Mum, amidst sobs. "Let's hope that the change of government will happen soon. We should all pray extremely hard for peace to return to Uganda."

"We certainly should pray very hard," said Mum, "and I'm very confident that we'll be able to meet again soon, my darling. Cheers to you both for now!" She said a teary goodbye to them and hung up the phone.

Chapter 5
Family Visits

After receiving news of the killing of her two brothers, the loss of her unborn baby, and the unfortunate death of her father, Helen was depressed beyond measure. The only thing she then preferred to do every day after work, was to go straight to the bedroom, lie on the bed and read until she fell asleep. She even was no longer interested in helping with household chores; Jonathan was left to look after the house as well as doing all the cooking. On many occasions, he found her in bed crying or just staring up at the ceiling. He got genuinely concerned about her and he tried to arrange various activities to cheer her up, but she was not interested in anything. He became increasingly worried about her health and well-being. He ran out of options of what to do to bring her out of her depression, and back to being happy and cheerful again. He ran out of options.

But one day he thought of something he could do, and which would be irresistible to her. 'A visit from her beloved mother will definitely do the trick; it'll bring her back to her old self,' he said to himself. 'I want to give her a surprise, so I want to arrange this without her knowledge. I am sure I can collaborate with her sister, Mary, on this. I know Mary will keep a secret.'

So, over the next few days, with Mary's help, Jonathan arranged Mum's visit, and truly, Mary kept the secret; she handled the arrangements on the Uganda side without the knowledge of her sister. She arranged the issuance of Mum's passport and flight ticket. Mum would fly out of Uganda on Saturday evening, arriving in London early the next day, Sunday.

Earlier that week, Jonathan managed to persuade Helen one evening to stay with him in the lounge, instead of going straight to the bedroom after work, as it had become her habit lately. He made the dinner and brought it on trays, so that they could have it together on the sofa. They had it in complete silence. After eating, he moved close to her and gave her a cuddle, and he hadn't done this for quite a while. He wanted to break the ice in preparation for delivering the news of Mum's forthcoming visit. He gently turned her head round so she would look into her eyes. He gave her a quick peck on her cheek, and when she didn't object, he kissed her passionately on the lips. Helen responded positively. With a big smile, he took her hand and said to her: "Come on, I'll take you to bed myself today."

He led her to the bedroom upstairs. By this time, she, too, was smiling a little. They sat on the bed, and he slowly undressed her and gently pulled her towards him. He kissed her fondly, and when she didn't resist, he pulled her closer to him and made love to her passionately. Helen, too, enjoyed it. This was the first time they made love since the loss of their unborn baby. And from then she seemed to be getting back to the cheerful Helen Jonathan always knew. He thought that the time was right then for him to talk to her about the visit. 'I must do it today," he told himself. "Possibly during dinner tonight.'

Helen made the dinner that evening and served it at the dining table. She placed Jonathan's plate in front of him, but after a while, she noticed that Jonathan was not eating his food; he was just turning his fork round and round around the food without eating any of it; after a few minutes, Helen turned to him and then said: "What's the matter, Jon? You're not eating your food, aren't you well, or don't you like the food I've served?"

"Oh no, darling," answered Jonathan. "I'm fine. Please don't worry about me." He slowly got up from his chair, walked over to her and stood behind her. He put his hands around her shoulders and quietly continued: "There's something I want to tell you, darling."

Helen was a bit puzzled. She quickly turned round to look into his eyes: "Yes? What is it?" she asked in a slightly raised voice. "I desperately want to hear it. Please, tell me; I am waiting."

"Darling, we'll be going to Heathrow Airport on Sunday morning to welcome a special guest," Jonathan announced, with a huge smile.

"Who?" Helen asked impatiently. "Please tell me!"

"Your darling Mum," Jonathan excitedly replied. "She's coming over to visit us!"

"What? That's not possible!" Helen screamed. "How come I didn't know about it? You're kidding me, Jon, aren't you?"

"No, I'm not," answered Jonathan. "You remember I told you recently that I was working late? I was not! I was secretly arranging the trip, and I'm afraid, with your sister, Mary's collaboration! I wanted to give you a surprise, and I wanted to cheer you up. The sadness from the horrendous and upsetting events we've been through has particularly weighed heavily on you, So, Mary and I have been secretly working on this. I must say, Mary has been an angel: she has brilliantly arranged everything for me at the Uganda side, and I am most thankful to her," He held his wife tightly and, after a short silence, said to her: "I hope I've managed to surprise you, have I?"

"Of course, it's a huge surprise, darling!" said Helen. "I don't know what to say to you and to Mary, the traitor!" She gave her husband a squeeze and a big kiss on the lips. "You have given me many surprises before, but this one beat all of them! I have no words yet to thank you." Smiling from ear to ear, she continued: "I promise I'll have my revenge for this one day. Just you wait!" She squeezed him more and gave him another big, passionate kiss.

"Your task in this, darling," said Jonathan, "is to make the second bedroom into a wonderful bedroom for Mum. I mean the best!" After a minute's silence, he continued: "We want her to have the best time of her life here with us. Poor Mum, she has been through a lot lately, and we must salute her for her resilience! But remember, darling, you haven't long to prepare a room fit for a Queen, our special Mum!"

"I promise I'll do my utmost, darling," responded Helen. "We want Mum to remember her first visit to our home and London always!" Looking lovingly into his eyes, she said: "May you be blessed always, darling! I love you to the end of the world!" She quickly stepped away, and with a wide smile, she performed a little dance as she cleared the table.

On the day Helen's Mum was due to arrive, which was a Sunday, Helen woke up early and excitedly got dressed, and woke Jonathan up early, too. They were soon ready for the journey to Heathrow Airport. Since it was a non-working day, there was little traffic on the road, allowing them to arrive well ahead of the plane's arrival time. They parked the car in the airport's lot and strolled leisurely to the Arrivals area. Joining the crowd of people waiting to meet their family and friends, they stood outside the Arrivals gate.

Waiting for Mum to come through, Helen was so nervous that she could not keep still; she held onto Jonathan very tightly and kept asking him to re-assure her that she was not dreaming. Jonathan squeezed her hand from time to time to confirm to her that everything was fine, including the long wait, which made her nervous. After what seemed an endless wait, Mum's small frame, with a head of graying hair, walked nervously out of the gate, holding her brown handbag tightly and pulling her suitcase behind her.

"There she is!" Helen said to Jonathan in a raised voice. She pulled herself away from Jonathan, walked quickly to the metal barrier, and unconsciously pulled at its joint to open it, and it gave way! She ran through the opening towards her Mum. "Mum, there you are!" she shouted as she got to her. She put her hands around her, almost lifting her off the floor.

"Welcome to London, Mum," she said, giving her a loving kiss on the cheek. With her left hand, she took the suitcase from her, and with her right hand, she took Mum's hand and led her to where

Jonathan was standing. She realised there was a barrier between them, so she walked with her mother towards the opening at the end of it. She walked towards Jonathan. Jonathan, too, was walking quickly towards them. They came together instantly, and with tears in her eyes, Helen said: "Jonathan, meet Mum, your mother-in-law, for the first time."

"So nice to meet you, at last, Mum," said Jonathan. "It's been a long wait, but it's been worth everything!" He embraced her warmly and continued: "Welcome, Mum. We're very excited to see you, and we're looking forward very much to take you to our humble home for the first time. This is a great moment I'll not forget!"

Mum looked him in the eyes, smiling widely and gave him a long hug and a kiss on the cheek and said: "This special hug is from my late husband, your late father-in-law. He was looking forward so much to giving you the hug himself, but alas, that was not to be. I am therefore giving it to you on his behalf." When she eventually released him, he took the suitcase from Helen, and they all started walking towards the car in the Airport parking lot, and they immediately started on the journey to their home in Hampstead, North London.

◆══════◆

Helen had brought an extra jacket, which she had left in the back seat of the car. She turned around to her mother and said to her: "Mum, please put that jacket around your shoulders to protect you from the cold London weather. You'll need to dress warmly until you get used to the cold UK weather. We don't want you to catch a cold. We'll take you shopping soon to get you some warm clothing in a few days' time after you've had a good rest."

"Thank you, Helen," her Mum said, picking up the jacket and putting it on. Settling in the back seat, she gazed out of the car window, marvelling at how close the numerous towering buildings were to the road. 'If this were Uganda, so many kids would be running into passing cars and getting killed,' she thought. 'I wonder how many accidents would happen in a day. Incredible!' She closed her eyes to nap but was soon disturbed by Helen's voice.

"Mum how is my dear sister, Mary?" Helen asked. "I can't thank her enough for handling your travel plans so efficiently, and without my knowledge. Can you imagine?"

"Mary is a superstar!" answered Mum. If she wasn't around, I don't think I would have managed to handle everything by myself. Poor girl, she is the only child I now have in Uganda. I almost lost her, too, when she became so distressed after the death of her father and two brothers, almost at the same time.”

“I agree with you, Mum,” Helen said. “Mary is a unique human being. Even when we were young and at primary school, she never let anybody bully me. She always went the extra mile to protect me, her young sister. I’m so glad I have her as my elder sister.” After a short silence, she continued, jokingly: “I do hope that her husband is as protective of her and her children as she was of me.”

“Her husband, Robert, is a wonderful man,” Mum said. “Mary and her children are lucky to have him. I say, as lucky as you are to have Jonathan! Of course, Robert is very protective of her and the children!”

“Thank you very much, Mum,” Jonathan remarked. “It’s very gracious of you to say so about me!”

Helen and her Mum continued chatting all the way as Jonathan carefully drove them along. Since it was quite early on Sunday, there wasn’t much

✦══════✦

traffic on the road, and they arrived home safely in less than an hour.

"Thank the gracious Lord, we are safely home," said Jonathan as he got out of the car. He quickly walked round to Helen's side to open the door for her. He also quickly opened Helen's mother's door and held her hand to help her out of the car: "Welcome to our humble abode, Mum," he said as he gave her a big hug. He then led the two ladies into the house.

As soon as they entered the house, Helen took her mother straight to her bedroom. "Welcome to your room, Mum," she announced. "I hope you'll like it and that you'll be comfortable in it."

"It's a very nice room, my darling," Mum said. Looking around it, she continued: "It's like a Princess's room. So beautiful. I love it, love it! I thank you and Jonathan for all the trouble you've taken to arrange my visit. I'm very proud of you both, and I'm sure we're going to have a super time together."

Helen showed her around the room; she showed her the wardrobe, the dressing table, and the bathroom. "I'll leave you now so that you can get organised and freshen up if you want. I'll go get the breakfast ready and I'll give you a shout when it's ready. In the meantime, don't hesitate to let me know if you need anything. See you soon."

Left alone, Mum walked around the room and admired everything in it, with a big smile on her face. She couldn't help herself from sitting on the beautifully made double bed. She pulled the duvet up slightly and looked at the soft, inviting linen below, and with mixed emotions, she said to herself: 'How I wish my dear husband was here with me to share this luxury with me, if only Idi Amin, the dictator, hadn't caused his untimely death by killing our two precious sons! I'm sure he'd have loved coming to London again with me to visit our wonderful daughter, Helen, and meet our amazing son-in-law, Jonathan. "He would be over the moon, no doubt!"

She walked over to the lovely dressing table at the bottom of the bed and looked lovingly at the flowers beautifully arranged in a tall glass vase placed on one side of the dressing table. She picked up one of the pink roses, sniffed it and held her breath for a while. Its soothing scent immediately brought back to her mind the exquisite decoration on the boat on Lake Victoria where Helen and her late fiancé Steven got engaged. She held the flower close to her chest and walked to the open window to look at the communal garden below. She stood still for a minute, looking at the roses in the garden, and again sniffed at the rose in her hand and said to herself: 'This reminds me of when Helen and her brothers and sister were little, running around the family garden in Kampala, back in the day, and their father sitting on the wooden garden chair watching over them. It was magical!' She smiled to herself for a moment but became sad again and said, 'Now my wonderful husband and my gorgeous two boys are all dead.' So sad!' She shed a tear as she walked to the bathroom to freshen up.

"Mum, breakfast will be ready in five minutes," Helen called out.

"Okay, Helen, thanks," Mum answered. "I'll be down shortly." She hurriedly changed into fresh clothes and walked downstairs to join Helen and Jonathan at the dining table for a hearty breakfast. They all enjoyed it tremendously.

Within a week of her visit, Mum said that she had had enough rest, and she was ready to go shopping for the appropriate clothing for the British weather. Helen arranged trips to take her to various

shopping centres and said to her that she would
have plenty of choices. The first place they went to
was Oxford Street in Central London. Although it
was the busiest shopping place in London, Helen
wanted her mother to have the experience of
navigating her way through the crowds of people
from the UK and from all around the world. Many
tourists had Oxford Street on their bucket list.

They got to Oxford Street quite early in the
morning, but crowds of people had already formed
in most of the shops. Mum could not believe it: she
stood still for a minute trying to take in the
situation, but she told herself that she had to get
used to it if she wanted to buy anything; she and
Helen should just push their way to get inside the
shops, as everyone was doing. It was strange and
funny to her, but she started enjoying it. There were
so many outfits to browse through and try on the
ones she selected. Although it was a pleasant
surprise for her, it was also quite exhausting.

"How do you manage to do any shopping in
crazy places like this one?" she asked Helen. "I
would be fainting every few minutes if this was my
regular shopping place."

"It would be impossible to shop here daily, Mum," Helen answered. "That's why I go to the smaller and cozy centres, which are also close to us. I purposely brought you here because I wanted you to experience this madness. Amazing, isn't it?"

"I agree with you, my dear: it's a mad but also amazing place," said Mum. "But I am glad you brought me here to see it with my own eyes. I will always remember it."

They slowly made their way through the throngs of people and managed to get to a few shops where they were able to buy Mum's appropriate clothing. Although it was summertime, she felt cold from time to time, and she needed warmer outfits. She was, however, completely knackered by midday. So, when they got to the Marks and Spencer store, Helen suggested that they go straight to the café for some refreshments and a well-earned break. Mum was pleased, as she desperately needed a cup of tea. Helen ordered one for her and pineapple juice for herself. She also ordered some carrot cake to accompany their drinks. Mum enjoyed the break very much.

Whilst relaxing in the café, Mum said to Helen: "I'm amazed that you don't spend all your earnings buying the brilliant things available in these shops. They are incredibly good, and many of them are reasonably priced. I am glad I do not live here permanently; I would get bankrupt within a week!"

"But you'd get used to it quickly, Mum," said Helen, "then shopping would quickly become a boring chore. However, I'm thrilled that you're enjoying the shopping and you're having fun. Jon and I wanted you to have a complete change from the horrid time you've been through lately. While you're with us, we want you to relax and get back to your previous self, happy, go lucky and always smiling, Mum, before you return to Uganda."

Mum suddenly became sad, and she covered her face with her hands and, in a melancholy voice, said: "Oh, Helen, please do not mention the word 'Uganda'. Whenever I hear it, I shudder! I want to forget the atrocities going on there while I'm here. I'm afraid the harassment and killings by the Government will get worse day by day. I won't be surprised if your sister, Mary, phones us today or tomorrow to report the killing of another close relative. This is now part of the daily life there." She paused and poured herself another cup of tea; she took a sip and then continued, "People in the country are very fed up with the Government, and I know that many people are contributing towards overthrowing it. I know for certain that there's already a group of people undergoing military training in the jungle in preparation for a coup. I've heard that the group is led by a young non-military man who is determined to acquire the necessary military experience to oversee the takeover. These boys and girls are so committed that we all believe that they will succeed. It baffles me that the Government hasn't any inkling about what's happening. I've also been told in confidence that some members of our extended family are among those who're undergoing training in the jungle. We must salute them! We all hope and pray that their efforts will be rewarded soon!"

"Wow, Mum, what interesting and amazing news you've given me!" remarked Helen. "Do you have any clue who these young fighters are?"

"No, but I can tell you one thing," Mum said. "Many of the families who have been directly affected by the Government's cruelty, such as ours, have been approached to offer financial support secretly." She looked around the café to make sure that there was nobody nearby who would be listening, and when she was sure they were safe, she continued: "And I have also personally already contributed towards this cause. I've used some of the money your late father left me, and I'm doing this in his memory."

"Good for you, Mum!" said Helen excitedly. "We'll all pray hard for the coup to succeed, and I have no doubt that it will!" They both sat back and hurried to finish their drinks. They then continued with the shopping until late afternoon.

A VISIT TO JONATHAN'S PARENTS

Soon after arriving in London, Mum mentioned to Helen and Jonathan that she wanted to meet Jonathan's parents soon. She requested them to arrange a trip to them sometime soon. She said she wanted to thank them for bringing up Jonathan so well and for acting as Helen's parents in the UK. She said that she could not wait to meet them face-to-face. She did not think that a phone conversation with them would replace the joy of meeting them in person.

"Of course, Mum," Jonathan said quickly. "I can't see why we cannot go to visit them this coming weekend. It's not a very long journey; if we go early in the morning, we could return home the same day. But, knowing my mother, she'd want us to stay for much longer; we can plan to return the following day. I'll give them a call tomorrow and see what their plans are for this weekend. I'm already looking forward to that!"

"So do we," Mum and Helen replied in unison, and they both laughed.

The following day, Jonathan telephoned his parent, and they all agreed that the coming weekend would be perfect for the visit. And as Jonathan had said, his mother wanted to have them for longer than one day. They, therefore, arranged for getting to Kent around midday on Saturday and then leave straight after lunch on Sunday. Jonathan's Mum and Dad were very excited and couldn't wait for Saturday.

When Jonathan relayed the information to Helen and her Mum, Mum got up immediately and, with a big smile, suggested to them that she prepared some Ugandan food before they went, and she would heat it up a Jonathan's parents' home and have it for dinner on Saturday. She would make easy-to-reheat food, which would be reheated when they got there. "I would like Jonathan's Mum and Dad to taste Ugandan food. What do you think?"

"That's an excellent idea!" Helen quickly said. "I'll help you to choose and make it before we go and then heat it up when we arrive. As you know, Jonathan, Ugandan dishes are perfect for this sort of thing. Once reheated, the dishes will be as good as newly made. What do you think, Jonathan?"

"That's brilliant," he answered. "As long as you include my three favourite Ugandan dishes, the 'matooke' mash (Ugandan green bananas mash), and Ugandan beef casserole (beef casserole cooked in banana leaves), and the special peanut sauce. I won't complain!"

"But, of course," said Helen. "A Ugandan feast will not be a feast without those three dishes, and as you know, they're all very easy to re-heat without losing the original flavours. So, Mum and I will go to the shops tomorrow to get the proper ingredients we need."

"I can't wait to see Dad's face when he tastes the dishes," said Jonathan. "He is always eager to try new foods. I'm sure he and Mummy will be blown away! I'll call Mum again to tell her what we've decided to do. She'll love it even more as she won't be making all the meals for the two days."

Helen, her Mum and Jonathan got up very early on Saturday morning, and Helen prepared breakfast speedily. They ate it fast so that they could start on the journey to Kent before the traffic built up on the roads. They were on the road by 7.00 am, and the roads were not busy. Jonathan and Helen shared the driving, and the journey was just a doodle. They arrived at Mum and Dad's house in Kent just after 10.30am.

Upon arrival, Jonathan's mother walked straight to Helen's Mum: "Hello, sister!" she said as she embraced her, giving her a loving hug. "What a pleasure it is to see you, lovely lady! We've waited for this moment for so long, but we're so happy that you're finally here. You're very welcome!"

She then hugged Helen and Jonathan and gave them a kiss, too. She led them into the house and Jonathan's Dad was eagerly waiting just outside the front door. He walked quickly to them, hugged each in turn, and with a wide smile said: "Please come on in; you're all very welcome, especially Mum, who we're meeting for the first time." He gave another hug to her, took her hand and led the way inside the house.

"Tea for everybody?" Jonathan's Mummy asked. Before anyone answered, she disappeared into the kitchen, and within seconds, she returned with a tray with the tea and a freshly made sponge cake. Helen quickly walked to her mother-in-law and said: "Please sit down. I'll now take over and serve the tea. She poured the tea and handed it to everybody, followed by slices of the sponge cake. They all had tea and cake while they chatted to each other.

After the tea, Jonathan's Mummy took Helen and her Mum upstairs to show them their bedrooms. Jonathan and his father remained in the lounge, chatting away to catch up on each other's news since they last met.

As Jonathan's Mummy, Helen and her Mum returned to the lounge, Helen leaned over to her mother-in-law and quietly asked: "Can you please show me where the kitchen is so Mum and I can get the dinner ready? Mum is anxious to have all the dishes properly heated up; she wants to ensure that it's at the perfect temperature when it's served."

Mummy led her to the kitchen, and she cleared the part of the worktop close to the cooker and asked Helen: "Is this enough space, dear?"

"More than enough, Mummy," Helen answered.

Mummy then turned to Helen, grabbed her, and with a wide smile, gave her a big hug, and while holding her tightly said: "We haven't met for a long time, so, can we please have a chat before you start heating the food? I miss you a lot."

"We, too, miss you and Dad very much," said Helen. "I wish we lived closer to you; I'd be spoiling you massively. I'll try to persuade Jonathan that we come to visit you more. I know both of us are very busy with our jobs, but we must find more time for you and Dad, our beloved parents!"

"That'll be great, darling," said Mummy. "I would have loved to be with you at the loss of your unborn baby, and when you received the very sad news of the death of your dad and your two brothers. That must have been very hard for you. But we're glad that Jon looked after you well through all this."

"Thank you Mummy," Helen said. "But as you said, my wonderful husband, Jon, was with me through it all, and to share all the sadness."

"I'll now leave you to get on with getting the food ready," said Mummy. "Dad and I can't thank you and your lovely Mum enough for making it for us. We can't wait to try it!"

"Thanks again, Mummy," said Helen. I'll now go get the food from the car so that my Mum and I can start heating it up."

"I'm sure it'll be very yummy," Mummy said as she walked back to the lounge.

"I hope so, Mummy," said Helen. "Mum can't wait to hear your comments on it afterward. I'll go get her so we can start organising the food. I'll see you shortly."

Just before dinner time, Helen and her Mum got very busy warming the food, putting it in dishes and spooning it into serving dishes. The lovely smells emanating from the food whiffed to the lounge, making the diners very hungry, and they just wanted to get to the table and tuck into it. As soon as everything was set up at the dining table,

Helen announced: "Dinner is ready, ladies and gentlemen. Please come to the table."

Without hesitation, they all took their seats at the table, and Helen's Mum started serving the food. As each dish was plated, Helen described each using both the Ugandan name and the English translation. The dishes were Beef 'Luwombo' (Beef Casserole Cooked in Smoked Banana Leaves), Steamed 'Matooke' Mash (Mash of Ugandan Green Bananas Steamed in Banana Leaves), Freshly Roasted Uganda Peanut Sauce, Lightly Spiced Roast Potatoes, and Steamed and Buttered Spinach.

They ate the dinner in complete silence; then Helen broke it, asking, "Is the food alright?" Her eyes scanned the faces around the table, searching for any sign of approval or dissatisfaction.

"Exquisite!" Jonathan's Dad answered with a big smile. "I may even request for seconds!"

"I agree with Dad," said Jonathan's Mummy. "It's a special meal!"

"I, too, agree," added Jonathan. "I've had this food before many times, but I still can't have enough of it. Well done, Mum and Helen. Amazing food!"

"I'm glad it hasn't been a disaster," Helen's Mum said. "I didn't know whether you would like it, and you loved it! Thank you!"

Jonathan's parents asked for second help, and Helen's Mum gladly served more food to them. "Unbelievable! But I'm so, so pleased!" she quietly said as she went back to her seat. She and Helen were very satisfied that the meal was a great success.

The following day, Jonathan's mother prepared a Sunday Roast, and they had it as an early lunch. Although it was totally different from what was served the previous day, it was also delicious, and everyone enjoyed it enormously. Almost straight after the meal, Jonathan, Helen and her mother bid farewell and started on their return journey to London. They had had a wonderful time in Kent with Jonathan's parents.

MUM VISITS BUCKINGHAM PALACE

Two weeks after her arrival in London, Helen's mother told her and Jonathan that she always wanted to go to Buckingham Palace. She said that she'd said to herself many times in the past that if she ever had a chance to visit London, she would not miss a chance of going to Buckingham Palace: she desperately wanted to see where her favourite family, the British royal family, lived.

One evening, when the three of them were relaxing in the lounge after dinner, she brought up the subject. "Helen, you know how much I love the Royal Family," she said quietly. "I wonder if it'll be at all possible for you to arrange for me a visit to Buckingham Palace, even if it's only seeing it from outside."

"Of course, Mum," Jonathan answered quickly. "We'll do our best to get tickets for that. But as it is summertime with a lot of tourists already in London, it may be a little difficult, but we'll try our best to secure tickets for you and Helen. As I'm still off work, I'll start checking straight away."

"I'm certain Jonathan will sort out something; he never wants to be defeated," said Helen. "It'll be amazing if Jonathan can carry this off; we'll just have to wait and see. If he does, I hope we'll even be able to take some photos of the Palace for you to keep."

"I can't wait!" Mum replied with a wide smile.

✦══✦

Two days later, Jonathan had great news: he'd managed to secure two tickets, but Mum and Helen would be part of the summer group touring parts of Buckingham Palace. He returned home with the tickets in his briefcase.

"Guess what, Mum," he announced. "You and Helen are going to Buckingham Palace this Friday! I've got the tickets for you!" He opened his briefcase and pulled out the tickets and handed them to Mum. "I'll take you and drop you two at the main entrance to the Palace; you'll then be told what to do. I'll collect you afterward. How about that?"

"Excellent, Jonathan!" screamed Mum as she hurried to hug Jonathan and get the tickets. "I just can't wait for Friday!"

For the next two days, Mum talked about nothing but the eminent visit to Buckingham Palace. She could hardly sleep at night; she was all the time only thinking of that visit. Helen and Jonathan were ecstatic to see how the forthcoming trip to Buckingham Palace made Mum so excited and happy. Helen couldn't thank Jonathan enough for arranging Mum's visit to the UK and now a visit to Buckingham Palace, too.

◆═══◆

The day of the visit to Buckingham Palace finally arrived. Mum got up very early, got dressed and went down to the kitchen and quietly prepared breakfast. She was humming 'God Save the Queen' as she got the breakfast ready. She checked on the weather through the open kitchen window and she was extremely happy to see that it was going to be a nice, warm summer day; it was perfect for the trip. After getting the breakfast ready, she just sat down at the dining table and waited for Helen and Jonathan to come down to have it.

"Good morning, Mum," Helen said as she walked to the dining table. "You're up very early today, and you've already made the breakfast for us all! Thank you, Mum. It's very sweet of you. We'll be able to leave for BP early."

"You're welcome. I just couldn't sleep any longer." said Mum, "So, I thought I'd get up and do something useful: get the breakfast ready. I'm glad we can start off for Buckingham Place early."

"Jonathan," Helen called out. "Breakfast is already at the table; please come down immediately. Our darling Mum has already made it, and it means we can start off for BP early."

"Okay, I'll be down shortly to join you," answered Jonathan. "You and Mum can start having yours."

After a hearty breakfast, Jonathan drove the two ladies to Buckingham Palace. It was a beautiful day; the sun was shining, and it was quite warm. Mum looked out of the car window and looked at the passing cars; she wondered whether any of them were also heading for Buckingham Palace. 'Maybe we'll meet some of them there,' she said to herself.

"What are you thinking of right now, Mum?" Helen asked as she turned round to face her.

"Nothing in particular. Just excited to be going to BP!" answered Mum. "My dream is coming true!"

"We're both very happy for you, Mum," Helen said. "Let's hope it'll be as exciting an experience as you hoped."

"I'm sure it'll be," Mum said. "I just wish Jonathan was coming with us. "I'd have liked to have a photo taken of the three of us at BP to show Mary and other relatives back in Uganda. I bet they'd all be very jealous!"

◆══◆

"Unfortunately, he can't join us," said Helen. "But don't feel sorry for him. He has been there two times previously. As a government employee, he has attended two of the Queen's Summer Garden Parties, and I was lucky to attend last year's party as his spouse.

"Okay, I now feel better for him," Mum said as she then relaxed for the rest of the journey.

Jonathan dropped them just outside the main entrance to Buckingham Palace, and Helen took Mum's hand and led her inside. She showed their tickets to the guard at the entrance, and they were handed their itinerary for the tour and were allowed to move forward. They joined the next tourist group to be taken around parts of the Palace by one of the Tour Guides. "This is it!" Mum whispered to Helen. "I wonder whether you're as excited as I am to be touring BP!" Helen just smiled and squeezed her hand tighter.

"Good morning, ladies and gentlemen," said the tour guide. "The summer tours of the place are conducted only when the Queen and her family are away, and the tours don't include the Queen's private area. You'll be shown only the public areas of Buckingham Palace. You'll be shown only the non-personal rooms of the Queen in the Palace. But they're all very interesting, and I'm confident that you'll enjoy seeing them. Please follow me."

The first stop was in the Greeting Room, where official visitors waited before they met the Queen. It was elegantly furnished and hung on the walls were portraits of some of the past sovereigns. Mum recognised Queen Victoria's portrait and pointed it out to Helen, smiling fondly. They then moved on to the Meeting Room itself, which had a large recent portrait of the current queen, Queen Elizabeth II; it had a soft light above it, depicting a calm and warm welcoming environment. Helen and Mum walked slowly around the room, noting the many impressive ornaments neatly placed around the room. The tour guide then led them to the main kitchen, which was very large with several cookers, at least a dozen fridge and freezers, and endless workstations, and large serving tables. Mum looked round the room and quietly whispered to Helen: "I wouldn't know what to do with all this space if it was my kitchen. It is a whole house for many people!"

They were next taken to the official dining room. It was a huge room and in the middle of it was an equally huge dining table and chairs, which would seat over 100 people.

"Wow, I feel sorry for the staff who would be serving the food here," Mum, again, whispered. "How would they keep the food hot for all the guests? Amazing!"

The tourists were then taken to the Investiture Room. It was small but was very cozily decorated and furnished. It gave the impression of being calm and inviting, and Helen and Mum felt the calmness. They walked close to the sovereign's chair and stood there for a few minutes admiring its workmanship: "Very impressive," Mum quietly commented. The group was taken to a few more rooms, which were all very impressive to Helen and her Mum.

Finally, the group was taken outside the Palace to see the neatly manicured gardens. The tour guide said to them that they could walk to any part of the garden but should return to the start point within 10 minutes. He told them that they could even take photographs in the garden if they so wished. Mum didn't hesitate to ask Helen to take some of her and some of them together. They walked to various parts of the garden quickly and took as many photos as they could.

"Everything we've seen is fit for a Queen, no doubt!" Mum concluded as she and Helen walked back to where the Tour Guide was waiting. With all the tourists assembled, the guide led them to the palace exit. "I hope you've enjoyed the tour of Buckingham Palace," he said to the group. "Goodbye and have a safe journey home." He then walked off.

When they left the Palace, Helen and her Mum walked to where they had agreed to meet Jonathan after their Buckingham Palace visit, and he was waiting for them in the car. As Mum chatted about the amazing things they had seen in Buckingham Palace, nonstop, as Jonathan drove them back home. Her glowing, happy face was a picture to see.

Whenever Helen and Jonathan managed to take odd days off work, they arranged further trips for Mum to other famous London landmarks during the remaining days of her holiday. They wanted her to have a lasting memory of her visit to the UK. She appreciated and was amazed at each of them.

CHAPTER 6
ANOTHER CHANGE IN UGANDA

The following Monday, Helen and Jonathan returned to work, leaving Mum alone at their house, but she did not mind that. While they were at work, she volunteered to take on housekeeping duties for them, including cleaning, ironing, and cooking. She made sure that dinner was always ready by the time they returned home. As she was now familiar with the area, she didn't mind going by herself to the nearest supermarket to get any ingredients she needed to make the meals. She took intense pleasure in doing these chores for her daughter and son-in-law as a small way of thanking them for the incredible visit they had arranged for her. The trip made her incredibly happy and more confident since the loss of her beloved husband and two sons, virtually at the same time. From time to time, however, she felt a little anxious thinking about the imminent end of her visit; very soon, she would be returning to Uganda, where her sad memories are gravely embedded. Nevertheless, having her elder daughter, Mary, and her family close to her was a great asset and helped to lessen the sadness. She was, therefore, determined to embrace the rest of her visit with positive emotions by making Helen and Jonathan the food they adored and looking after them the best way she could.

During one of their after-dinner chats, Mum said: to Helen and Jonathan: "Can you please tell me for certain that you will visit me in Uganda as soon as normality and peace returns? I have a strong feeling that the change of Government will happen soon."

"We will indeed do, Mum," Helen responded. "Won't we, Jonathan?"

"Yes, of course," said Jonathan. "We haven't stopped praying for the return of peace and security in Uganda; we're sure the Lord is listening, and He will answer our prayers soon."

"Once you let us know that the change has occurred, we'll get on the plane like a shot!" Helen said excitedly.

✦═══✦

"I'll be the happiest Mum in the world, and I'll then be able to reciprocate your hospitality and goodness," Mum said, smiling.

Mum's flight for her return journey to Uganda would be at eight o'clock in the evening of next Friday, six weeks after her arrival. So, to take her to the airport, Jonathan and Helen left the house as soon as they returned from work at the end of the day. They wanted to make sure that they got to the airport in plenty of time so that Mum wasn't rushed. And so, they did. As the flight was going to be punctual, they led her straight to the check-in desk. She checked in promptly and she was ready to continue to the departure lounge. But before she moved on, she put her hands around them and said to them: "I cannot thank you enough for what you have done for me. You've turned a sad woman, who I was when I arrived soon after the death of my husband, your dad, and my two sons, your brothers, into an incredibly happy and more confident woman. I'm sure the three of them are all looking down at us now, with big smiles on their faces, and shouting: 'Cheers to you three!'" She gave them a hard squeeze and continued, smiling widely: "I can't wait to see you in Uganda soon so that I can 'revenge' your hospitality, as Idi Amin would say!"

She turned around and slowly walked to the departure gate. Just before she went inside, she turned to look at them and she gave them a goodbye wave, smilingly weakly, and then went inside the gate.

Jonathan looked into Helen's eyes, and he saw tears running down. As he hugged her, she quietly said to him: "Thank you very much, darling, for making Mum so happy. She won't forget her time in London soon!" She held his hand, and they slowly walked towards the car park, got into the car, and started on the journey home in silence.

Before she left the house for the last time, Mum had made sure that she prepared for her daughter and son-in-law one of their favourite dishes, leaving it in the oven at a very low temperature to stay warm. When they arrived back and opened the front door, a glorious smell of Mum's cooked dinner embraced them. They looked at each other, and, smiling widely, they hugged tightly, and Jonathan quietly said to Helen: "At least we have your Mum for one more evening, even if it's only in her food.

We deserve that, don't we?" They both laughed. They immediately had the food, and they enjoyed it tremendously. Jonathan pointed his hands in front of him and said: "Well done, Mum," Jonathan shouted. "You're, indeed, a special Mum and a superstar! God bless you!"

The following day, Helen's sister, Mary, telephoned to let Helen and Jonathan know that Mum arrived back home safely. "Helen, Mum is a completely different person to the one I drove to Entebbe Airport six weeks ago!" she said. "I almost didn't recognise her when she walked out of the airport! You've made her an incredibly happy lady, indeed. She can't stop talking about all the exceptional things she did with you two and the amazing places you took her to. You've made her life worth living again. I thank you sincerely!"

"Thank you very much for letting us know about Mum's return. It's nice to know that she got back safely. As you already know, we would love to come over to visit you all," Helen said. "But you know very well what we're waiting for." She was referring to the anticipated change of Government, but she didn't want to spell that out on the phone just in case someone hacked the phone and was listening in. "Mum told us that you'll let us know when the time's right for us to come."

"Definitely, we will let you know, and we hope and pray that it'll be soon," said Mary.

"We hope so, too, Mary," Helen said. "But we'll be waiting anxiously. In the meantime, we pray that you all keep well and safe. You, Mum, and your family are all very special to us."

"Thank you, Helen. I'll pass the message to Mum and my family," Mary said. "I know they will appreciate your concern and care! Goodbye for now, Helen."

A few weeks after her return to Uganda, Mum phoned Helen and said, "Your friend, Martin, has contacted me to ask for your telephone number; he said he wanted to speak to you urgently. Is it okay to give it to him?"

"Of course, Mum," Helen answered quickly. "You know how I owe my life to him. I wouldn't be here now speaking to you if it wasn't for him. I'm very intrigued about what he wants to say to me. He'd said to me that he would only contact me in an

emergency. I wonder what the emergency is. I'll
await his call anxiously."

"Okay, I'll let him have the phone number
asap," Mum said. "However, to change the subject,
do you remember what we talked about while
having coffee at the M&S café in London? Things
are now moving speedily. Just keep your fingers
crossed! We still need all your prayers."

"I do understand," Helen said. "But don't
worry, we're all praying for that every day."

"I better hang up now, dear, so that I can call
Martin to give him your phone number. Bye!" Mum
hung up the phone.

A few minutes after Mum's call, Martin
phoned: "Hi Helen, you won't believe this, but I'm
phoning you from Nairobi!"

"Why, what's happened? Why are you in
Nairobi?" Helen asked impatiently.

"My crazy uncle turned against me, too, and so
I had to run for my life!" said Martin, almost
choking. "He accused me of being too friendly with
the people he considers to be against him, mainly
the lawyers and medical doctors, and those who he
says are spreading lies about him, both at home and

abroad. He specifically mentioned your family. He said that you and your late brothers, among others, were planning to overthrow him. He said that I was ganging with his enemies, the wrong crowd. So, he told me to watch out before I got into serious trouble. He also asked me to provide him with the contacts of all my friends and acquaintances, both at home and overseas, so that he could deal with them 'properly,' and you know when he says things like that about anyone, he means having them killed! I became very concerned and worried about you, especially as I know that his spies have already discovered where you are now. I'm sure he would not hesitate to send his gangs to abduct you. That's why I thought I should warn you so that you can alert the UK police about this and make sure you don't go to isolated places.

"You know you are very special to me, as are your remaining family here and your friends in Uganda. Please rest assured, I would never betray anyone. However, there are many others who might, for money. I don't want anything unpleasant happening to you, your family or friends. That's why I'm ringing now to ask you to take extra care. I'm sorry to be giving you this worrying information, but I thought you should know and should be prepared for any eventuality. As you know, knowledge is power."

"I appreciate your continuing concern about my welfare, Martin," said Helen. "As I've said to you before, you're, indeed, a special friend, and I'm privileged to be one to you. I thank you very much for all you did for me previously. I wouldn't be alive today if it wasn't for you. You put your life on the line for me, and that's very courageous. I don't know how I can ever pay you, Martin, but you're always in my prayers. I'm so glad you managed to escape; otherwise, you could be a goner! You, however, need to be on the alert all the time. Nairobi is very close to your uncle, should he wish to chase you.

"As regards my safety here in the UK, please don't worry about that. My husband will help me with alerting the police about the possibility of my abduction by Amin's gangs. I doubt that any such grotesque plans would succeed here. I promise you I'll be very careful with my movements. Thank you so much for taking the trouble to advise me. How do you plan to protect yourself, Martin?"

"Possibly move to the USA. As you know, I studied and graduated there. Thereafter I stayed there and worked there for a couple of years. I'm sure it won't be very difficult to go back there and hopefully get a job there again. It will be very difficult for my uncle to extract me from there. I'll be on the lookout for his gangs; I know what they look like and how they behave. Don't worry, my dear. I'm sure I'll be safe in the US."

"I'm glad you're making plans to move on," said Helen. "The further away you go, the better for you."

"Thank you, Helen," Martin said. "But before you go, I thought I'd let you know what I heard is happening underground in Uganda. I've been told, and I have concrete evidence that it is true, that groups of young, professional men and women who are fed up with my uncle's murderous rule are secretly undergoing military training at various locations in the jungle around Uganda and are planning to overthrow the government. Before I left Uganda, it was confirmed to me that the takeover was imminent! Isn't that great news? I personally think so!"

"Very exciting news indeed, Martin, "said Helen, pretending to be hearing it for the first time. "When do you think this will happen?"

◆═══◆

"Maybe in a couple of months," Martin said. "I would like to help them if I can, as I think that'll be best for the country. I hope, though, that my uncle would not be killed. What I think is that he would arrange to leave the country as quickly as possible to avoid being captured. I know he is a coward deep down!"

"Very interesting news you've given me, Martin. Thank you." Helen said. "Please keep me updated on any developments, and please keep yourself safe; we need people like you around all the time."

"I'll, indeed," said Martin. "Goodbye, for now, Helen. Please make sure you, too, keep yourself safe."

Almost to the time, Martin predicted, the Guerrilla Army assembled and secretly and quietly moved to Kampala in the middle of the night. From a long distance, and with immaculate assistance from the locals around the country, the Guerrilla Army secretly formed an armed circle around the Command Post, Idi Amin's official residence. The civilians living within the circle had been warned about what was about to happen, and they had been asked to stay away from their houses for that night.

As most of the civilians, particularly those living in and around Kampala, had become so fed up with Idi Amin's rule, they were ready to assist the underground army in any way they could to get rid of him and his henchmen. So, the preparations for that evening went perfectly, and the Guerrilla soldiers were in their allotted locations early that evening, waiting for their Commander's orders via walkie-talkies.

On the dot of midnight, the soldiers were ordered to quickly but quietly move close to the Command Post and start firing at it at the same time. All those stationed within the armed circle around the Command Post obeyed and they all rushed forward, firing at the Command Post from all angles. They took Amin's soldiers guarding the residence by surprise. With bullets raining on and around them, they were in disarray and didn't know which way to run. Many of them were hit by the oncoming bullets and they were all falling to the ground dead like flies! Within a few minutes the Guerrilla soldiers had reached the residence. They forced their way inside, shooting everyone in sight. Some of these soldiers reached Amin's bedroom, determined to arrest him. But as soon as he heard the commotion, he jumped out of the bedroom window and hid in a bush outside. Luckily for him, he wasn't found, and he managed to escape and eventually leave the country.

The Guerrilla Army also surrounded the Parliament Building, the Broadcasting House, and many other important Government buildings in Kampala. As the guards at the different buildings were taken by surprise, they could not offer much resistance; they just abandoned their locations and ran away. The Guerrilla Army managed to take control of all these buildings without much resistance, most importantly the Broadcasting House.

By early the next morning, the Guerrilla Army had taken possession of almost all the Government and State buildings with minimal resistance. They also managed to replace most of the old regime's personnel guarding the buildings with their soldiers. Although there was some firing noise in Kampala during the night, it wasn't loud enough to alert the general population that a major change in the country was taking place or to wake them up. The takeover only came to light when the Guerrilla Army leader came on the radio early the following day to announce the overthrow of Idi Amin and his government.

"Ladies and gentlemen and honourable citizens, the long-awaited new change in the leadership and governing of our country has finally happened," the head of the Guerrilla Army announced. "At last, the brutal President, Idi Amin Dada and his corrupt henchmen have been overthrown. You will no longer be oppressed by them. We can now say goodbye to the random arresting and murdering of innocent citizens. You will soon be informed of your new Government. Long Live Uganda!"

Without waiting for the new leader to continue with his address to the nation, almost everybody in the country, apart from Idi Amin's cronies, burst into loud cheers! They ran out of their houses to the streets, joyfully shouting and singing praises to the new leader. Almost all the streets and roads in the country were filled with people singing, drumming and dancing in praise of the new leader. 'You've saved us from the murderer,' such chants could be heard. 'May you be blessed forever!' one loud chant was heard. No one was addressing the new leader by name, as the excited audience hadn't waited to hear his name properly during his address. The audience was only interested in hearing that Amin was no longer their ruler! By late morning, people around the country had organised street parties, and a lot of food and drink were handed out to the gatherings, free of charge. They were unbelievable spectacles, and they were replicated in most parts of the country.

Later that day, Helen's sister, Mary and her family went to Mum's house to share the excitement and jubilation. An instantaneous party was thrown; it was attended by family, friends and neighbours to celebrate the demise of Idi Amin's despotic and murderous rule. By that time, the new ruler's name was now widely known and was being chanted by every peace-loving Ugandan. His name was Emmanuel Magara!

"Who knew the end of the brutal rule would occur so peacefully!" Mum said amidst happy tears. "May the gracious Lord bless Emmanuel Magara, our saviour!"

Mary embraced her and excitedly said: "Can we phone Helen now and tell her of the great news?"

"Yes, darling," Mum answered. "I know she must have heard it already from their bulletins, but it would be lovely if she could also hear it directly from us. Let's do it right away."

Mary then phoned Helen: "Hi, Sis, I know you must have already heard the news, but Uganda is now free of the murderous dictator Idi Amin! We're now at Mum's house, celebrating the moment! Everywhere in Uganda, people are having house and street parties. The size of crowds attending these parties is unbelievable; the scenes are exhilarating! We all wish you and Jonathan were here to celebrate with us."

"Yes, darling," said Helen excitedly. "The removal of Idi Amin was in the UK news on the television and radio broadcasts last night. We couldn't believe it, but we're extremely happy about it. I feel very pleased that the small contributions I sent to the Guerrilla Army have been part of this amazing liberation! Long live General Emmanuel Magara!

"It's, however, sad that we're not there to join in the celebrations. Please celebrate more on my and Jonathan's behalf and of course, in memory of our late Dad and late brothers Denis and Phillip. Of course, we'll be celebrating with you in spirit."

"We know you'll be, Helen," said Mary. "But hold on, Mum wants a word with you."

"Hi, darling," said Mum. "We never expected the change to occur so quickly, but there you are! We hope we're now in a free, secure and peaceful country."

"We can only hope so, Mum," said Helen. "But I have a feeling it's going to last for a long time."

"Let's enjoy it while it lasts," Mum said. "When will you be coming to visit us? We can't wait to see you in a free and happy Uganda!"

"Jonathan and I are already talking about it," answered Helen. "But, between you and me, I want the journey to Uganda to be a surprise to Jonathan; I'll book the tickets without his knowledge. So, if you next phone us, and he answers the phone, please don't mention it to him. However, all will depend on how quickly we can take leave from work, bearing in mind that we took quite a bit of it during your visit not so long ago. We hope that our employers will be kind enough to approve our next leave without a problem soon."

"Okay, Helen," Mum said. "We'll wait for your call to let us know when you're coming over. But hold on, how could Jonathan not know about it? You will have to synchronize the leave dates with him. You may have to think again."

"I think you're right, Mum," said Helen. "My plan is possibly a non-starter."

"Think about it, darling," Mum said. "Regards to you both. Bye!"

"But hold on, Mum, before you go, can you please tell me briefly how the takeover happened, and happened so peacefully?" Helen asked

"It's a very long story, which I'll tell you when you come over." Mum responded. "However, we must thank Emmanuel Rugara and his Guerrilla Army; they put their lives on the line for our freedom, and for a very long time!

"Many young men and ladies voluntarily joined the Guerrilla Army and sacrificed their comfortable life, and some of them their studies, to go into the jungle to train as soldiers. They were all, like all of us, fed up with Amin's brutal rule, and many of them had had relatives and friends murdered on Amin's orders, of course! They thought that joining the Guerrilla Army was a small price to pay, and the only way to gain freedom from the dictator!

"Some of us contributed financially to the Army's upkeep in the jungle, including me, as you know. We thought that was the least we could do in pursuit of freedom, and in memory of our murdered relatives and friends.

"We'll talk about it more when you come. Okay, dear?"

"Very well, Mum. I'm eager to hear the whole story," said Helen. Goodbye for now, Mum. Love you!"

CHAPTER 7
TRIP TO UGANDA

Helen contacted their usual Travel Agent to check out possible travel dates, and she realised that it would be impossible to confirm the dated without Jonathan's involvement. So, the 'secret' plan would not work. Her best option, therefore, was to insist on paying for the tickets herself.

One evening, while they had their dinner, Helen said to Jonathan: "Darling, how do you fancy a trip to Uganda a month from this Saturday?"

"Oh, darling, I don't' think we can afford it yet," he replied. "We've spent quite a bit lately. Before thinking about that, we need to do some saving. Don't you think so?"

"Yes, my dear," Helen said. "Saving is what I've been doing. I'll be buying the air tickets for us, and the Travel Agent has given me possible travel dates a month from now.”

Jonathan stood up quickly and said: “What? You, naughty girl!” He went over to her and gave her a hug and a big kiss on the lips. “But you didn’t mention it to me before; why?”

“It is a surprise!” Helen said with a big smile. “It’s my turn to surprise you. You’ve given me quite a few surprises yourself before.” She squeezed him and returned his kiss on the lips.

“Thank you so much, Sweetie!” said Jonathan. “Indeed, you’ve given me the biggest surprise of all! Do I have to do anything?”

“Yes, darling,” Helen answered with a huge smile. “You can apply for a three-week’s leave. Can you do it asap because I want to confirm the travel dates with the Travel Agent and pay for the tickets.”

“I promise I’ll apply for the leave tomorrow,” he said.

After collecting the tickets from the Travel Agent, Helen phoned her Mum: “We’ll be coming on Sunday, a month from now, for three weeks!” she said. “I have the tickets in my hands!”

◆══◆

"Oh! Helen," Mum said loudly. "What wonderful news! I can't believe it. But why only three weeks?"

"I'm afraid that's all the leave we can take now. You remember we took some leave when you came over to London not so long ago. Will three weeks be okay with you?"

"Oh! Helen, any time will be fine with me," Mum answered excitedly. "The fact that you now can travel to Uganda again is extremely good news for me. I still can't believe it's true! I can tell you now I won't be able to sleep at all until your arrival; I'll be too excited! I'm going to give Mary and her family the great news immediately, and I know that they'll want to start making the programme for your visit right away. I can't believe that I'll soon be able to reciprocate the love, kindness and care you and Jonathan extended to me during my London visit."

"We, too, are very excited and are looking forward to seeing you again very much, Mum. In the meantime, please stay well and healthy."

Mum gave the wonderful news to Mary and her family, and they were all overjoyed. They promised to make Helen and Jonathan's visit an occasion to truly remember. Mary's kids, Jane and Michael, could not hide their excitement over seeing their favourite aunt again soon and meeting their uncle Jonathan for the first time. There was joy all around as everybody waited for their guests' arrival in a month's time.

Jonathan's excitement over his forthcoming trip to Uganda was for all to see. He couldn't fathom that he would be on his very first trip to Uganda, and for that matter, to the whole of Africa! He couldn't wait to break the news to his parents. At the weekend, he phoned them to let them know. They were equally excited, and they spread the news to all their relatives dotted around the UK, their friends, and all their neighbours.

"Wow, son," his mother exclaimed. "What a lucky boy you are!" she said. "How nice that Helen is funding the trip! How many people get chances like that: travelling to such exotic destinations? I must say, Helen is an exceptional lady, isn't she? You two are so good for each other. Dad and I see you two as an incredible power couple, and we both adore both of you immensely."

"Mum, that's very generous of you to say!" said ecstatic Jonathan. "We'll be gone for only three weeks, as that's all the leave we can take now. But be sure, Mum, that both of us will be thinking of you and Dad all the time. And please don't worry about us while we're away; we'll be in very good and safe hands with Helen's family. We, too, love you and Dad very much.

For their trip to Uganda, Helen and Jonathan would be flying with British Airways from Heathrow Airport in the early evening of Saturday, arriving in Entebbe early morning on Sunday. For safe keeping, they left their car at the Airport's 'paid long stay' car park. The travel procedures at the airport went smoothly, and the flight took off on time.

During the flight, Helen and Jonathan opted to watch the films that were on offer, and they stayed awake all the way. On landing at Entebbe Airport, they both felt a little tired. Jonathan was very excited as they disembarked; his ever first visit to the continent of Africa! As they walked down the steps from the plane to the tarmac, Jonathan couldn't believe how beautiful the country was and how pleasant the weather was. He could see the sun rising over the horizon: it was an amazing and perfect circle of bright orange colour. He almost tripped over the steps, gazing at it. He was also struck by the cool and gentle breeze that hit him straight in the face. He was gob smacked! He had expected the weather to be very hot, humid, and uncomfortable. But he enjoyed the short walk from the plane to the Airport building.

"Is the weather always like this in Uganda?" he asked Helen. "If so, I might consider moving to Uganda permanently, with you, of course!"

"We're very lucky to have arrived in very good weather," Helen replied. "It is not always like this; it gets quite warm as the day goes on, and it can get hot and humid, particularly in the afternoons. I don't think it would be a good idea to move here permanently. I wonder whether you'd feel the same in a couple of days' time. I think it's still very early days for you to think so."

As they walked to the Airport building, Jonathan stopped from time to time to admire the scenery around the airport, and he admired every direction he looked in. He smiled all the way to the Airport building.

The scene inside of the building, however, was different: not so pleasant. There was chaos everywhere. Almost all the furniture was broken and thrown everywhere, the walls were dirty, with the paint peeling off in many parts, and the carpet stained and torn in many places. Helen was sad and upset; the place was different from what it was when she left Uganda. 'This must be a result of Idi Amin's Government neglect and mismanagement,' she said to herself. 'He and his cronies didn't carry out any maintenance to the building at all. It looks very disgusting!'

As it was only their plane that had arrived at that very hour, there weren't many passengers queuing for passport checks and baggage collection. So, they got through quite quickly and exited the building speedily.

On getting out of the Airport gate, they immediately saw Helen's Mum at the front of the group of people at the meet-and-greet area. Helen could also see her sister, Mary and her husband, Robert, standing not far away. The three of them walked forward towards their guests, with Mum leading. She put her arms round Helen and Jonathan and kissed each one on the cheek. She held onto them for a while and not letting them go. She then looked into their eyes and, with a broad smile, said: "Welcome to Uganda, you two. You're here in Uganda at long last!" Pulling Jonathan's hand and raising it up, she introduced him to Mary and Robert. Jonathan gave Mary a big hug and whispered in her ear: "Hello, Mary, my partner in crime!" He was referring to their secret collaboration in arranging Mum's trip to London without Helen's knowledge. They both laughed cheekily. He then shook Robert's hand: "So nice to meet you, Robert," he said to him, smilingly. "Your wife gave me immeasurable help when I needed it previously. She's a superstar!"

They then all walked to Robert's car, got in, and started on the journey back to Kampala and straight to Mum's house.

Mum led the guests to the lounge, and before they sat down, Mary's children, Jane and Michael, who were hiding behind the sofa, jumped up and ran to their Auntie Helen and threw their arms round her. After a little while, Michael moved away a little, but Jane held on, and with a wide smile, she said loudly: "It's so, so nice to see you, Auntie! We missed you terribly, and we thought you'd gone away for good and that we'd never see you again!" She squeezed her Auntie's hand very tightly and pressed her head against her body.

Helen gently pushed her away slightly and had a good look, staring at her with admiration: "Me too, Jane. I'm very delighted to see you both. But you've grown so much: you're almost as big as me, Jane!" She pulled Michael closer to her and added: "And so are you, Michael, you are not far behind!" She gave them both a huge hug. "I missed you two very much, but I'm so glad I'm here with you now."

Jonathan, Mum, Mary and Robert looked on, all smiling. "Come and meet your Uncle Jonathan," said Helen as she led them to Jonathan. "I know you're going to have a lot of fun with him."

"So pleased to meet you two at long last," said Jonathan. "I've heard so much about you from your Auntie Helen; she talks about you constantly. We are going to have a lot of fun together, won't we?"

Mum then led Jonathan and Helen to the settee, and sitting between them, she said: "May I now formally welcome you to Uganda? You're going to be spoilt rotten while you're here. It's the 'revenge' I promised you after you spoilt me so much during my visit to you in London. You better be prepared!" She then went with Mary to the kitchen to get some drinks for the guests. Soon after, Mary returned with the drinks for everyone, with Mum following.

While they all enjoyed their drinks, Jonathan said, smiling widely: "Thank you very much, Mum, for the generous welcome. My wife and I are very privileged to be here with you in beautiful Uganda. I'm sure we won't mind the excessive weight we will gain whilst here, through the indulgence you've warned us about. When we return to the UK all our family and friends will know that we'd had a great time here!"

"And I'm certain Jonathan and the kids can't wait to start having fun," Helen added. Isn't that so, Jon?"

"But, of course!" Jonathan answered emphatically

After the drinks, Mum asked Mary to take Helen and Jonathan to their room, just in case they wanted to freshen-up before breakfast. She herself went back to the kitchen to assist the house-helper to speed up the preparation of the breakfast. It was soon laid out on the dining table. It looked like a huge buffet meal rather than just a breakfast!

"Come on, all of you," Mum called out. "Please come and help yourself to whatever you fancy."

Laid out on the table were loads of fried eggs, sausages and bacon, and slices of toast. Also, there, were steamed tomatoes, baked beans, and orange, and pineapple juices, freshly made. The guests went round the table to choose their food, in complete silence. They all returned to the lounge with their plates of food, sat down and tucked into it again in silence. They all enjoyed the food enormously.

"You were right, Mum," said Jonathan. "We're being totally spoilt. We've no doubt that we'll gain a lot of weight, but that is a very small price to pay for the fun we'll have eating your gorgeous food!"

After breakfast, Helen and Jonathan went to their room, and Helen went straight to have a leisurely bath, after which she opted for a nap, but she was all out for the rest of the morning. Jonathan went back to the lounge to chat to Mary and Robert, but when Mary noticed his eyes starting to close, she urged him to go and have a little snooze, too. He did so immediately, willingly.

The following day, Helen wasn't feeling very well; she had a headache that wouldn't go away. From time to time, she also felt hot and cold, and became nauseated. So, the best she and Jonathan could do was to take that day easy. He was eager to get Helen better sooner than later. They spent that day mostly on the front verandah and outside in the garden, sitting in the shades the trees provided. They had brought books with them and so, did a lot of reading.

Mum and her helper made light meals for them, which, although Jonathan enjoyed very much, Helen did not have much appetite for it. She preferred to just sit quietly and read. The following day, she was still not feeling very well, and she wanted to continue taking it easy. By this time, Jonathan was getting more concerned about her health. He said to himself: 'If she isn't 100% by tomorrow, I must get medical help for her.'

Luckily, by the third day, she was feeling a lot better, and she was eager to start showing Jonathan parts of Kampala. She wanted to start showing him parts of the City Centre. Her sister, Mary, kindly offered to drive them around as she was off work for a few days. She warned them that there wouldn't be much to see as most of the buildings were still in a dilapidated state, following years of mismanagement and destruction by Amin and his gangs. She drove them passed several buildings that were magnificent and attractive in the olden days. Many of them were now derelict. Most of the damage had occurred after Helen left Uganda, and, therefore, she couldn't believe the amount of damage that had been inflicted on the city. Most of the once-popular restaurants and cafés had either closed or had been destroyed, and it was very difficult to find any place to go to if you wanted to go out for a meal or a drink. A few hotels, though, were still operating.

When Helen and Jonathan wanted a break in the touring, Mary drove them to the Nile Hotel to have a drink. Before Helen left Uganda, Nile Hotel was a five-star hotel and was one of the most popular places for overseas tourists to stay, and as such, it was almost full all the time. When they went inside, Helen couldn't believe how dilapidated the hotel had become. At the bar, almost every drink they asked for was unavailable. They were served either bottled soft drinks or plain water. So, the three of them ordered bottled Coca-Cola.

As they drank their Coca-Cola, Mary asked Helen if she wanted to take Jonathan to see her old University, Makerere University College. "I'm warning you, though," Mary said. "It's very different from the University you graduated from; most of it is in a sorry state. You won't believe what it has become, my dear. I know you'll get very upset when you see it."

"No, Mary," Jonathan said quickly. "I wouldn't like Helen getting upset. I want her to remember her university as it was when she attended it. Isn't that so, darling?"

"That's correct, Jon. I'd be extremely hurt if I saw it in a derelict state," she answered. "Let's skip that, Mary."

Helen, with Mary's assistance, continued to arrange other interesting tours for Jonathan during the rest of their visit to Kampala. They wanted to show him the Royal Palace of the Kingdom of Buganda, in particular. The King who resided in it was known as 'Kabaka,' and the Palace was known as 'Lubiri' in Luganda, the language of the Baganda. The Baganda comprised of a large tribe owning and living in the southern part of Uganda where Helen and her family came from. In the olden days, the Palace was a spectacular place, and the story was that it had been modelled on Buckingham Palace, albeit on a much smaller scale.

During the political upheaval in Uganda, the new rulers wanted to take over the Palace and they fought the then King (Kabaka), forcing him and his family into exile. The exiled family was granted asylum in the United Kingdom, where the King sadly died many years later. The new rulers in Uganda didn't value the status and importance of the Palace, and without proper maintenance, it got into a state of disrepair. It was badly damaged inside and outside, and all the traditional and historical items were looted. After Amin was overthrown, the Kingdom was re-established, and the late King's body was returned to Uganda for a proper royal internment in his Kingdom. His heir was installed thereafter.

With the Buganda Kingdom re-established, the Baganda people were determined to assist the young King in resurrecting the Palace and rebuilding it to its former glory. Wherever they were, many people from Buganda contributed towards the re-building of the Palace, brick by brick, and to re-establish its Royal status. This ambitious project took some years to get the Palace to a respectable state, befitting the new King's royal residence.

Helen had previously related the story of the Palace to Jonathan, and whilst in Uganda, her Mum showed him some old photographs of the Palace as it was previously. Although it was still undergoing restoration, Helen thought it would be a good idea to show it to him, so that he could get a sense of what it would be like when completed.

At the start of the rebuilding of the Palace, many people, particularly from the Baganda tribe, were very interested in following its progress as well as relearning its history. So, some historians from the region gathered information on the Kingdom's history and information about the previous Kings, and their pictures. They got a temporary structure erected next to the building site, where the compiled material was exhibited and where some Baganda elders with relevant knowledge volunteered to talk about the subject to the visitors who wanted to hear it. Gradually, the structure became a place of interest to many people, including tourists.

When Helen and Jonathan visited the Palace building site, they were keen to listen to the talks and to look at the old pictures of the Kings and to purchase souvenirs to take home. After the talks, they were also allowed to walk around the nearly completed sections of the Palace. Jonathan was astounded by its size, and he could clearly see that it would be a magnificent building. He turned to Helen and hugged her.

"Indeed, it used to be a magnificent and grand Palace before it was destroyed." said Helen, "I know that a lot of people, including my family, can't wait to see the whole building completed and back to its former glory. I'm sure it's going to be a very impressive place when it is finished. I'd love to come back, of course, with you and visit it when it's completed."

"And so would I," said Jonathan.

After touring the Palace site, Jonathan held Helen's hand, looked into her eyes, and, smiling broadly, he said: "What a magnificent tour you and your sister Mary arranged for me! I can't thank you two enough." He gave her a big hug and a loving kiss.

The following day, Helen was feeling poorly again, and she remained in bed until late. Jonathan and Mum were getting more worried about her. Mum suggested getting medical help, and Jonathan agreed. She contacted a doctor she knew very well, and who was a colleague of her late son, Philip. He agreed promptly, and that same day, Mum and Jonathan took her to the hospital where he worked, Mulago Hospital, in Kampala. He examined her and arranged for blood and urine samples to be taken for checks. After sending the samples to the hospital laboratory, he asked Helen to wait in the reception. She went and rejoined Jonathan and Mum in the hospital reception. An hour later, the doctor walked over to them and sat next to Jonathan.

"The samples have been tested," the Doctor said, looking at Jonathan. "I have studied the results, and I'm pleased to tell you that there's nothing wrong with your wife."

"So why does she become poorly from time to time?" asked Jonathan. "Can you please advise us what we can do to help her?"

He looked at Jonathan and stayed silent for a while. With a big smile, he said to him quietly. "She is expecting a baby! Congratulations, you and Helen! When the pregnancy is at an early stage, sometimes it's difficult to connect any illness to it. I think that's why she didn't work it out, until now. However, my advice is she should have plenty of rest."

Jonathan looked at the doctor and, in a surprised voice, said: "That's excellent news, Doctor! Isn't that so, Helen?" He pulled her up, wrapped his arms around her and gave her a big hug. Still holding her close, he continued: "We should really be ashamed of ourselves; why didn't we think of that?" He looked at Helen and gave her a big kiss. Turning to the doctor, he went on: "We both thank you very much for seeing us so quickly and for this news, of course!"

In excitement, Helen turned to the Doctor and gave him a big hug, smiling ear to ear, and said: "I'm very excited too, Doctor, and I also want to say a big thank you to you for giving us this wonderful news. We're both very thrilled!"

"We'll make sure she gets plenty of rest, won't we, Mum?" Jonathan said as he turned to her. She embraced both of them lovingly and said: "I'm so pleased I'll be getting another grandchild soon. In that case, promise me that you'll come back to Kampala soon after the baby is born, to introduce him or her to me. Is that agreed?"

"No question about that, Mum!" Jonathan answered quickly, still smiling broadly.

"Congratulations again to both of you," the doctor said to them and patted them on the back. "I wish you both a safe journey back to London." He waved goodbye and walked off.

Only three days remained until Helen and Jonathan's visit ended, which made Mum a little sad. However, she and Jonathan made sure that Helen had plenty of rest, as the doctor had recommended. So, they decided to cancel the last trip Mary had planned for them. It was to be a trip to the source of the River Nile, the longest river in Africa. It was situated just outside Jinja town in Eastern Uganda. Jonathan didn't want to go without his wife; he wanted to stay with her to look after her. They decided to take it easy during the last days, mostly sitting out on the verandah or in the garden, either reading or enjoying the scenery.

Jonathan kept thinking of Helen's over-excitement at seeing and going around the Palace site. This picture of Helen's excitement kept coming to Jonathan repeatedly. The interest she showed bordered on obsession. He wondered why this was so; he would discreetly speak to Helen's Mum when Helen was having one of her naps. So, one afternoon, when Jonathan and Mum sat on the balcony chatting, Mum unwittingly and casually mentioned that her late husband, Helen's father, was a close relative of the late King (Kabaka).

"A close relative of the King?" Jonathan, totally flabbergasted, asked. "What does that imply,

Mum? Does Helen then have royal blood in her?"
Mum, embarrassed that she let that slip, didn't
answer. After a while, Jonathan continued: "If that
is so, how come Helen had never, ever intimated
that to me, even jokingly? If she's, indeed, related
to the Buganda royal family, and she'd never
mentioned it to me, she must be surely an extremely
modest girl. What a secret to keep! If it's true,
Mum, I'm very proud of your daughter, and I'm
very privileged to be married to her! Can I talk to
her about it and praise her for her modesty?"

"No, no, Jonathan," Mum responded loudly and
quickly: "Please don't mention it to her. I know my
children very well: they don't want to talk about it.
That's how their father, too, wanted it to be. It
should be kept to themselves as they don't want to
be treated differently. I'd rather leave it to her; if she
ever decides to tell you, please let it be her personal
choice. Okay, Jon?"

"Right, Mum, I do understand," Jonathan
replied with a chuckle. "What a modest and
amazing daughter you have? I admire her highly.
And thank you for alerting me not to blub about it.
I'll keep the family secret; don't worry."

◆═══════◆

CHAPTER 8
ANOTHER BIG CHALLENGE

The Visit to Uganda was ending, and Helen and Jonathan's flight back to London would be in the evening of the next day, which was a Saturday; it had already been confirmed. During their last hours, Mum continued to fuss around Helen, making her eat the food she believed would keep her healthy during the pregnancy and help the baby to develop well. She advised her to continue eating that food even after she returned to London. Although she was feeling quite sad already about the imminent departure, she decided to make them a farewell dinner and invited Mary and her family too. It was a somber dinner as they all knew that that would be their last dinner together for quite some time. They ate mostly in silence. After the meal, short farewell speeches were made by Mum and Mary, and they and the other attendees wished them a safe journey back to London. Mary's children shed a few tears.

On Saturday afternoon, Mary's husband, Robert, arrived at the house in plenty of time to drive them to Entebbe Airport, accompanied by Mum. Mary didn't want to go with them, as she didn't want to show her sadness over her only remaining sibling and her husband's approaching departure. Although there was heavy traffic on the road, Robert managed to get them to Entebbe Airport 45 minutes before departure and Mum and Robert were able to spend a bit more time with Helen and Jonathan before they boarded. However, in a few minutes' time, they were asked to proceed to the appropriate gate for boarding. The plane take-off was on time, and the flight was comfortable.

The plane landed at Heathrow Airport on time, early morning on Sunday, and Helen and Jonathan proceeded through the arrival checks; they were amazed that the whole process was so speedy and that they were out of the Airport in no time. They went straight to the 'Long-Stay' carpark where they had left the car before they travelled three weeks before. They quickly got into the car and were soon on their way back home to North London. Much as they had enjoyed their three-week visit to Uganda, more so, seeing Helen's Mum again, they were happy that they would soon be back to their own home, which they both adored immensely.

While on the road, Jonathan said to Helen that he couldn't wait to get her home and spoil her totally; he wanted to make sure that their expected bundle of joy was developing well and that it would be delivered safely.

"The first thing I'll do when we get in the house is to run a nice bath for you," said Jonathan. "I know you love and enjoy a leisurely bath. While you're having your bath, I'll make you a nice cup of tea. How about that, darling?"

"I'd love that a lot, my dear," answered Helen. "And I'll make you one of your favourite meals tonight. I also want to spoil you from time to time. Please think hard about what you'd really fancy tonight and tell me before we get home."

"I'll let you know soon, my dear," said Jonathan. Darling, since the traffic light is green, I'm going to drive quickly so we can get home sooner."

He increased the speed and raved on. Helen shut her eyes, and within a minute, she fell asleep.

Jonathan got to the roundabout, which he would drive past going straight on. He was supposed to stop just before driving past it to continue straight ahead. He checked the roads coming to the roundabout from all sides, but when he could not see any vehicle approaching, he was confident that it was safe to drive straight on without stopping. As he was just a few inches from the roundabout, he saw a large truck approaching from the right-hand side at very high speed. The truck, too, didn't stop and was racing towards his car. He immediately realised that there was no way he would avoid a collision.

"Oh no we're going to crash!" he shouted. "Wake up, Helen! Darling, we're going to be …! Before he finished the sentence, the truck hit his side of the car with such force that he was flung forward, hitting his head hard against the steering wheel and the front of the car, almost splitting his head into two. A lot of blood gushed out of his head. He was left flopped against the steering wheel, and unconscious.

Jonathan's screams woke Helen up immediately and she, too, screamed: "Aaah! What is hap….?" But before she, too, could finish the sentence, her safety belt flung open and she was thrown about the inside of the car, leaving her crouching in the tiny space between her seat and the dashboard, with blood running from her broken left arm and leg, which were broken in many places. The car toppled and rolled down a slight slop, only stopping lying on its side against a concrete wall by the roadside. The truck driver didn't stop to see what damage he had caused; he just drove on, at high speed.

One gentleman, David Walters, who was driving past, saw the smashed car lying against the concrete wall. He got out of his car immediately and ran to the damaged car to check on the occupants. He noticed that there were two people inside the car who appeared badly injured, and there was blood everywhere. He quickly opened the driver's door and saw Jonathan slumped motionlessly over the steering wheel. He checked his pulse, but there was no beat. He then ran to the passenger door and saw Helen crouched on the floor, motionless, too. He checked her pulse, and, thankfully, there was a beat. He immediately phoned the Ambulance Service and reported the accident, and he was pleased to see the Ambulance vehicle promptly arriving. Three Medical Assistants jumped out, carrying their equipment bags, and ran to the damaged car.

"Thank you for coming so quickly," David Walters said to them. "There are two gravely injured people in the crashed car. I was driving along this road when I noticed the car. I stopped immediately and ran towards it to see if there was anything I could do to assist the occupants. The man and woman in it are both motionless, so I checked their pulses, and I'm afraid there was no beat in the man's pulse. There was, however, a beat in the lady's pulse. Could you please check them to see what you can do for them?"

The Ambulance staff then carried the two passengers from the damaged car to the Ambulance for examination. David stood by the Ambulance door and waited for what they would say. After a few minutes, one of the Ambulance Assistants came to the door, still pulling off his rubber gloves. "I'm sorry the gentleman is already dead," he said to David. "He even has gone cold already. However, we think the lady is still alive, though she's seriously injured and is currently in a coma. We'll take them to the hospital straight away for the Doctors to examine them further and to decide what should be done next. But thank you for stopping to help them; you're a great 'Good Samaritan'!"

"That's very kind of you to say," said David. "I'm glad they will soon be in great medical hands. I thank you again for your quick response." He went back to his car to continue his journey.

The Ambulance drove Helen and Jonathan to St Thomas' Hospital, which was the nearest Hospital, and handed them over to the medical team. At the Hospital, it was confirmed that Jonathan had, indeed, died from the injuries sustained in the crash. However, the team was encouraged to see that Helen was still alive, although still in a precarious state.

As soon as she was laid in the Hospital bed, Helen started bleeding heavily. At first, the team thought that she had a heavy monthly period, but they soon realised that it was more serious than that. Helen was having a miscarriage! One of the doctors dealt with the issue, and he later confirmed that Helen had had a miscarriage whilst in the coma. The team looking after her were very saddened: poor Helen had just lost a husband, and now her baby, too! The nurses, who were now in tears, thoroughly cleaned her and the bed, and they made sure she was comfortably sleeping despite being in a coma. They couldn't imagine how she would take the news when she woke up: she would be inconsolable! The medical team's priority, however, was to do whatever they could to get her out of the coma. The nurses frequently checked on her condition and took readings of both her heart and pulse beats, which were so far fine; this was reassuring.

Helen and Jonathan's next of kin were informed of the car crash in which Jonathan died and Helen was badly injured. As Helen had no immediate family in the UK, her employers were informed. The Chief Executive at her workplace and her work colleagues were beyond sadness over Helen's serious injuries and her husband's death. They decided that they would visit her often at the Hospital when she came out of the coma and when she was allowed to receive visitors.

On hearing the news of his death, Jonathan's mother collapsed and fell to the ground. While wailing uncontrollably, she said: "I can't believe that my one and only loving, charming and clever son is no more. How will I survive without him? He was our only reason for living. He is irreplaceable!" Her husband, Jonathan's father, took her hand and gently pulled her up. He put his arms around her and gave her a tight and loving embrace. With tears running down his face, he said to her: "That was

God's will, my darling. He decided to take our beautiful son to heaven, and he's now sitting comfortably at His side. I'm sure he is looking down at us with his usual big smile, asking us to be brave. We must, therefore, be strong and brave in his memory; he's in God's safe hands! Our priority now, darling, is to pray hard for our lovely daughter-in-law, Helen. We want her to recover from the extensive injuries she sustained. Don't you agree?"

"I do agree, darling," she replied. "I hope she will come out of the coma soon because I want to see her, cuddle her, talk to her; I want to share the immense sadness with her. Poor girl! I can't imagine how she'll process the news of the death of her beloved husband and, of course, our amazing son, Jonathan. As we always said, they were the perfect power couple, and they were inseparable!"

Jonathan's parents travelled immediately to London to arrange the repatriation of his body to their home in Kent for burial.

Helen's mother in Uganda was extremely devastated upon getting the news of the extensive injuries her daughter, Helen, had sustained and going into a coma, as well as the news of the loss of

her son-in-law, Jonathan. She couldn't believe that
the immeasurable happiness she, Mary and her
family had with Helen and Jonathan in Kampala a
few days ago was replaced by the indescribable
sadness of Jonathan's death and Helen's grave
injuries. Having lost her husband herself, as well as
two sons not so long ago, in quick succession, made
this news more unbearable to her. She prayed
incessantly for Helen's recovery.

'If Helen, too, dies, God forbid!' Mum said to
herself. 'I can't imagine how hard that will hit me.
Surely, I can't lose another family member this
soon. Absolutely unimaginable! But I haven't much
choice now but to travel to London to see what I
can do to assist my daughter's recovery.'

Helen's Mum, therefore, travelled to London
immediately to be close to Helen. She went straight
to St Thomas' Hospital, where Helen was being
looked after. She spent all the following days by
Helen's Hospital bed, and she spent all the time the
Hospital allowed her to stay; she talked to her
constantly, hoping that if she heard a familiar voice,
she would be urged to wake up from the coma. She
did this day after day.

During the third week of Helen's coma, Mum decided to concentrate on talking about her and Jonathan's recently ended visit to Kampala. She made sure she mentioned their visit to one of Helen's favourite places, the Palace of the King of Buganda (the Kabaka's Lubiri) in Kampala. For the next few days, she spent a lot of time talking about this subject over and over. And this did the trick! Suddenly, Helen opened her eyes, and she looked straight into her mother's eyes and said: "Hi, Mum, you're here! So nice to see you! Where's Jonathan? I'm surprised he's not here fussing over his unborn baby: he's always stroking my tummy and listening to the heartbeat." Mum didn't know what to say to her, so she just got up and leaned over Helen's face and then placed her hands on either side of it.

"You may not remember, darling, but you were both severely injured in a horrible car accident," Mum said, smiling weakly, "And you were both brought to this Hospital for treatment. I understand that Jonathan is being treated in another ward. You've been in a coma for over three weeks! You've just woken up this minute!"

"Oh, been in a coma, really?" said Helen, surprised. "I vaguely remember the accident; I hope our baby is okay, though."

You're being looked after by an amazing team of Doctors and Nurses at this Hospital. I'm sure they'll talk to you about Jonathan and the baby. Alright, my darling?"

"Fine, Mum. Thanks," said Helen. "I hope that will be soon."

"I better let the nurses know that you've woken up. They'll be elated, and certainly, they will want to come and speak to you immediately, my darling," Mum said just before she left. Helen closed her eyes again and immediately went off to sleep, but this time it was a normal sleep.

Mum ran to one of the nurses and, with a big smile on her face, said in a loud voice: "Helen is awake! Is awake!"

The nurse smiled broadly and said to Mum: "That's a miracle, isn't it? Let's go to her immediately!" The nurse followed Mum back to Helen's bed, but she was still sleeping soundly. The nurse checked her pulse and listened to her heart. She turned to Mum and said, with a smile: "She's now in a deep sleep: a well-earned normal sleep! Let's not disturb her. Please call me when she wakes up and we'll get her something to eat, she must be starving! It's wonderful news that she's out of the coma. You must be so relieved!"

When she woke up, the first thing on her mind again was to know where Jonathan was. She remembered that her mother had mentioned that he was in a different ward.

"Mum, now that I'm fully awake," she said, "can the nurse take me to Jonathan's ward? I'm desperate to know how he's doing."

"Darling, can we please first concentrate on getting you better and stronger first?" Mum responded. "Don't forget that you've just come out of a long coma, and you're still very weak. I would like you to have something to eat first; you must be starving."

Mum then went to let the nurse know that Helen was awake again and that she was now ready to have something to eat. The nurse returned with a tray of some soft food and handed it to Mum, saying: "I'm sure you'll be able to help her with it."

When Helen said that she could feed herself without assistance, Mum excused herself and went to the corridor to make a call to Helen's mother-in-law, Mrs. Taylor. She updated her on Helen's progress. She also wanted to discuss and agree with her on how Helen should be told about Jonathan's death. After some discussion, they both agreed that Mrs. Taylor should be the one to break the sad news of Jonathan's death to Helen. They, however, thought it would be more appropriate for a nurse to let her know of the miscarriage. So, Mrs. Taylor volunteered to travel to London the following day to pay a visit to Helen and gently break the news of her husband's death to her. On the way back to Helen's room, Mum stopped at the nurses' desk and requested one of them to join her in the afternoon of the following day to tell Helen about the miscarriage, and the Nurse willingly agreed.

When Mum returned, Helen had finished eating, and she was sitting in bed propped up against the wall. She was aimlessly looking out of the window at the blue sky. She smiled at Mum and said: "I badly needed that food, and I feel much more alive after taking it. Thank you, Mum, for arranging it and, of course, for caring for me so brilliantly. I'm sure having you around is aiding my recovery massively. You're a great Mum!"

"Thank you, Helen," Mum said. "I'm so glad you're getting better day after day." She sat down on the bed, took her hand, stroked it gently and kissed it lightly. She then said: "By the way, you'll be getting an important visitor tomorrow afternoon."

"Who, Mum?" Helen asked eagerly.

"Your loving mother-in-law, Mrs. Taylor, will be coming to see you tomorrow. She wants to know how your recovery is proceeding."

"Excellent news, Mum," Helen said. "I'm sure she'll also be able to take me to see Jon. Can't wait!" Mum didn't say anything more. She was feeling sick and sad about not being able to tell her daughter yet that her husband was dead and that she had lost the baby, too. She could not anticipate how the meeting would go the following day.

When Mrs. Taylor, Jonathan's mother, arrived the following day, she went straight to Helen's bed and gave her a long, loving hug, and she held onto her for a while. When she eventually released her, she said to her: "Dad and I are so sorry to know about what you've been through, but we're both very glad you're recovering well. Dad has sent his best wishes to you, and we both hope and pray that you'll be discharged soon." By this time, Helen's Mum was nervously standing at the foot of the bed,

◆══════◆

wondering how the conversation was going to go. The Nurse had also joined them in the room.

"It's so nice to see you too, Mummy. It's been a while," said Helen. "But first, how is Jonathan? Which ward is he in? Will we be allowed to see him? I'm very anxious to know how he is. I miss him terribly, and so is his unborn baby."

Everyone in the room stayed quiet, looking away from Helen, and the Nurse had tears in her eyes. "What's the matter? Everyone is so quiet. Please, Mummy, say something," Helen pleaded, looking intently at her mother-in-law.

Jonathan's Mummy placed her hands on Helen's shoulders, looked straight into her eyes, and in a shaky voice, with tears running down her face, said to her: "Darling, I don't know how to say this to you. I'm afraid Jon, your husband and my son, is no longer with us. He didn't survive the accident. He was injured very badly, and sadly, he died instantly at the scene of the accident," She then broke down and wept. With tears running down her face, she put her head on Helen's lap, face down, and in a muffled voice, she continued: "But we're all very thankful that you survived, and we still have you with us." She got up, walked to the Nurse

◆═══◆

and asked the Nurse to get closer to Helen's bed:
"This kind Nurse will update you on your unborn
baby."

Helen just froze, and she couldn't say anything.
She remained in the position she was in, propped
against the wall at the back of her head, staring
blankly ahead. Instantly, a river of tears ran down
her face and onto the bed, wetting the front of her
gown. Her Mum walked around to join her mother-
in-law and the Nurse and then asked the Nurse to
tell her about the baby. The Nurse moved close to
Helen, sat on the bed, held her hand and calmly told
her about her miscarriage, which happened whilst
she was still in the coma. Helen didn't move or say
anything; she remained frozen, with tears still
running down her face. By this time, Mum, too, was
sobbing. She sat on the bed and threw her arms
around her daughter, and they both wept. For the
next few minutes, there was complete silence in the
room, with everybody sitting on the bed with all
their hands on Helen, to try and console her. Helen
then looked at each in turn, blankly and in silence.
As they all started to open their mouths to say
something to her, she signalled them to stay quiet.
As she continued to stare ahead blankly, she said in
a weak voice: "I don't know what is going to

happen to me next. Tragedy after tragedy!" She then pulled the bedsheet over her head and continued to weep. The other three ladies in the room looked at each other, not knowing what to do or say next. The Nurse excused herself and left the room.

✦══════✦
217

CHAPTER 9
WHAT NEXT?

After two months in the Hospital, Helen was discharged, but her left leg and arm were still in plaster. She would return to the Hospital in one month's time to have the plaster removed. So, her movement was restricted. Her loving Mum, though, decided to extend her stay until her daughter was able to look after herself when she was alone at the house. She kept in touch with Helen's parents-in-law, and she wanted to be advised about Helen's late husband's funeral. They decided that it wouldn't be held until Helen had the plaster removed and feeling a lot better.

Since learning of her husband's death, Helen became introverted: she didn't want to speak to anybody or about anything. However, her mother was there for her; she diligently looked after both Helen and her house. She tried as much as possible to make Helen's favourite dishes, although Helen didn't eat much of the food, and they often ate in silence. Almost every day, Helen excused herself from the table halfway through the meal, went to her bedroom, watched a bit of Television and then went to sleep. This went on for several days, but Mum decided not to talk about it; she realised that Helen needed time to reflect on and process what had happened to her alone and in her own time. She would get back to normal life when the time was right and on her own terms.

When she had been home from Hospital for two weeks, the Chief Executive and the Human Resource Manager at her workplace wanted to pay Helen a visit. They wanted to find out how her recovery was progressing and to discuss the timeframe for her return to work. The appointment for the visit had been made a few days in advance, so Helen had a few days to prepare for the meeting. She was excited about this, and she asked her Mum to help her get ready for it. Mum was pleased to see Helen coming out of her bubble and beginning to converse with her normally.

"This will be an exciting day, Mum," Helen said with a faint smile. "I can feel it, and I'm looking forward to the meeting very much! I think

I'd like to put on a nice dress and have a little make-up on as well. Can you please assist me with all these?"

"Of course, darling, I will do anything you want," answered Mum. "Just tell me what dress you want to wear and the make-up products you want, and I'll get them ready for you. I'm also getting excited for you. I've even had the first smile from you for quite a while. It's great! What refreshments do you want me to put out for the guests?"

"Tea and coffee will do, Mum. Thanks," said Helen. "Your special sandwiches will be a nice addition."

"Will do," said Mum. I'll give you a shout when the doorbell goes."

"Thanks, Mum."

After getting ready and making herself comfortably seated in the lounge, the doorbell went. Mum opened the door, introduced herself and led the two visitors to the lounge where Helen was seated. The Chief Executive, quite a big man, gave Helen a long bear hug, softly saying to her: "I'm very, very sorry for what you've been through. We've all been thinking of you and praying for you." He gently pushed her away from him slightly and, looked at her from head to foot and continued: "But I can see the prayers are working; you're almost back to the beautiful, cheeky Helen we always knew!" He turned to Mum and said: "And thank you very much for looking after her."

The Human Resource Manager also gave her a hug and said: "It's so good to see you recovering well and we can't wait to see you back at work, but 'when' is the reason we're here today."

"I appreciate your visit very much," said Helen. "But please sit down first and let my mother spoil you a little with a nice cup of tea and her legendary sandwiches."

They sat down, and Mum served the tea and sandwiches she'd made.

While they were having the tea, the Human Resource Manager said: "Helen, we're here to find out from you when you think you will be able to come back to work, days or weeks. You may re-start on a part-time basis on your return to see how well you cope. But this won't mean a reduction in your pay. Our wonderful Chief Executive here has kindly agreed to the arrangement."

"How kind of you to suggest that!" Helen exclaimed. "I have been seriously thinking about returning to work since my discharge. I've been toying with the idea of returning soon after the plaster has been removed. I'd like to return to work then, and I'd like to resume working full-time. The only thing I won't be able to undertake, perhaps, is going on sole overseas trips. If I'm going with another person, I think I'll be okay. I may need help to move around until my limbs get fully strong again."

"That'll be no problem, Helen," the Chief Executive jumped in. "We'd love to see you back at work, and we promise we'll assist you in any way possible. We want you to know that we value your services."

"Just give me a call when the plaster is removed," said the Human Resource Manager. "Then you and I will agree on the exact date for your return."

Helen was now looking down with a few tears running down her cheeks: "I thank you very much and greatly appreciate your kindness and concern," she said without looking up. She pulled a tissue from the tissue box beside her to wipe away her tears; she then looked at the visitors, who were standing up by then, ready to leave. "Goodbye, Helen," said the Chief Executive. We look forward to seeing you back at work soon." They waved goodbye and left.

Helen raised up her right hand, which wasn't in plaster, and waved it from side to side, and with a cheek-to-cheek smile, she said to Mum: "Didn't I say it would be a good day? Not only a good day but an excellent day, hasn't it?"

"It has been a wonderful day, my dear," Mum said. "And when you're comfortably back at work, maybe I can then start thinking of going back home. I've been away for quite a while."

"Yes, Mum, I'm sure by then I'll be able to manage almost everything on my own," Helen said. "As you already know, Mum, I am a survivor!"

On the Monday following the removal of the plaster from her limbs, Helen went back to work. On entering the office building, she got handshakes, hugs and kisses from work colleagues, the Receptionist at the main entrance, the Lift Operator, the Messenger distributing the morning mail, and each occupant of the offices she walked past, to her secretary sitting just outside her office. Most of them gave her wide welcome smiles, and some shed happy tears. She was overwhelmed and gob smacked! She went into her office, and she saw two vases of beautiful flowers in the office, with *'Welcome Back'* cards attached to them. She walked over to them and smelt the flowers, and she couldn't stop tears filling her eyes. She quickly said to herself: 'Don't cry, Helen; no one will want to see you crying. Whatever you're feeling, please keep a wide smile on your face. That's what all your colleagues want to see.'

Her Secretary, Monica, was following behind her, and before she sat down, Monica grabbed her and gave her a hug and a peck on the cheek. "Welcome back, boss," she said. "We all missed you terribly. But we're so glad to see you back. I and all your colleagues in the office have decided that we'll not talk about any of the horrendous things you've been through. We want you to get back to the happy, cheerful Helen we always knew. If you want anything, please do not hesitate to let me know."

"Thanks, Monica," Helen responded. "I greatly appreciate that. But I'll be alright, I promise, and we're going to get back to our hardworking ways right away, won't we?"

"We will, boss!" Monica said, giving her boss a cheeky salute. "I'll go and get you some tea now." With a very big smile, she walked out of the office.

With all the kindness, love and devotion her work colleagues showed her, Helen found it relatively easy to settle back into the work routine. Their actions of love and affection showed her how much she was valued, and that was very humbling to her.

Among her duties was to arrange interviews for new staff for the head office, as well as the Company's overseas branches. Waiting for her on her desk was a thick file of applications for a job that had been advertised for a short-term Marketing Consultancy position at the Company's Nairobi office. The applicants should have extensive experience in Marketing, and the duties would involve developing, devising and recommending a Marketing Policy for the Company's branches in three East African countries: Kenya, Uganda, and Tanzania. Helen was, therefore, required to go through all the applications and prepare and have the shortlist of applicants ready by Friday to be able to decide on the final list of applicants to be interviewed in two weeks' time. With over 400 applications to go through, Helen had to work late on at least two days that week to meet the deadline, and she did. Having just returned to work after a three-month absence and still feeling a bit woolly, she patted herself on the back to have achieved this. The interview was arranged to take place in two weeks' time, and Helen would be one of the members of the interview board. She would be collecting the interviewees from the waiting room to the interview room.

One of the interviewees, James Jones, was the third interviewee. Helen went to collect him from the waiting room, as she did with all the interviewees.

"Good morning, Mr. Jones," Helen said. "Please follow me."

"Good morning, Madam," responded James Jones with a wide smile. He was tall, handsome, and very smartly attired. "I'll certainly follow you." Helen led him to the interview room.

"Welcome, Mr. Jones," said the Chairperson. "Please sit down," He sat down, facing the six Interview Board Members opposite him.

◆═══◆

The interview started with the Chairperson asking James to talk through his education, work experience and what he considered to be his relevant experience for the job in question. He confidently answered the question, as he did with all the questions put to him by the Board. When Helen put her question to him, he looked at her steadily and, with a faint smile, answered her question, confidently. At the end of the questioning, the Chairperson asked him if he had any questions for the Board. "No, thank you," he answered. "Everything is very clear, thank you for asking."

"You'll soon be informed of the outcome of the interview, Mr. Jones," the Chairperson said. "You may leave now." He left the room immediately.

All the Board members thought James Jones' performance was excellent, and they all voted for him to be appointed. He was subsequently appointed and was informed that Helen Taylor would be his contact point at the Company. Helen sorted out everything for him, and he travelled to Nairobi shortly after to start the job.

As was with all the overseas appointees, James Taylor was required to give a debrief to the Company at the end of the contract. Although he had been asked to contact Helen to make the appointment for him for this, he decided to go personally to Helen to make the appointment for him. He went to Helen's office one Monday morning, arriving soon after the offices opened.

"Hello, Mr. Jones," Helen said when he entered her office. "How did everything go in Nairobi? Did you like the place? It's a place I personally hold fondly in my heart."

"I had a nice time in Nairobi," answered James Jones. "It is a lovely place; I loved everything there, and I'd want to go back there for a holiday one day."

"I'm glad you liked the place," Helen said. "I'll now take you to my Senior Manager, Paul Duncan, for the debriefing meeting. Between you and him, a decision will be made as to where you'll be posted next if the debrief goes well, obviously, that is. Alright?"

"Yes, Mrs. Taylor, I'm ready," said James Jones as he got up. "But before we go, may I please ask you something?"

"Yes, what is it, Mr. Jones?" Helen asked.

"May I please take you for lunch today after I've done the debrief, if that's okay with you?" James Jones asked.

"What?" asked Helen, greatly surprised.

"Please, please!" pleaded James Jones.

Helen was quiet for some time and then said: "Okay then, but why?"

"I just want to thank you for all the help you've given me since I applied for the job," said James Jones. "I know it's part of your duties, but you've handled everything with great care and feeling, and I do appreciate that very much."

"Thank you for the compliment," said Helen. "You're welcome to come back here after your debriefing, and then you can let me know where you want to take me for lunch. We break for lunch at one o'clock. Is that okay?"

"That'll be perfect," said James Jones, with a big smile.

CHAPTER 10
ANOTHER NEW BEGINNING?

James Jones' meeting with Paul Duncan finished one hour before his lunch appointment with Helen. So, he decided to walk to a nice French restaurant he had been to before, just a street away, to book a table. He did that and then walked back to Helen's office to collect her. They were seated at their table by one o'clock.

Helen was a little nervous when they sat down for the meal. She thought: 'I hope this is just and only a truly thank you gesture from this gentleman, and nothing more serious than that. I've already sworn myself to a life of celibacy for the remaining years of my life as I've had enough heartache already.'

As they were looking at the menu sheets, James Jones put down his and looked at Helen. He was still looking at her when the waiter came to take their orders. Helen quickly told the waiter what she wanted, but her host hadn't decided yet; he was preoccupied with staring at her. Not wanting to waste time, he turned to the waiter and said: "I'll have the same as the lady is having." And the waiter went to get the food.

"Can I call you Helen?" James Jones asked. "I's so formal calling you Mrs. Taylor all the time. And please call me James."

"Okay, okay," Helen answered with a little grin. 'Here we go again!' she said to herself. 'I'm not ready for this, really!'

"You're a wonderful and very helpful person, Helen," James said, leaning over the table towards her. "I noticed that you go the extra mile to help people and make their lives easy. You certainly did that for me. That's very rare in modern-day offices. That's why I wanted to say a special thank you to you by taking you out for lunch today."

"I'm very flattered, James," Helen said. "I just do my job the best I can. I'm grateful that people such as you appreciate it. Thank you very much."

◆══◆

The waiter returned with the first course of their meal. "Please enjoy," he said as he walked away. They ate the food in silence. But before the waiter came back with the next course, James stretched his hand towards Helen and said: "Please, can I shake your hand?"

"You can," Helen said. "But I don't understand."

"You're a special lady if you don't mind me saying so," said James. "Thank you for being you!"

Helen sat up and slowly pulled away her hand. She looked blankly at James, then said: "But you've just seen me a few times, and only at work. How can you know that?"

"People will always know a genuinely wonderful person immediately they see one," James responded. "When I met you for the first time at my interview, I saw and knew straightaway that you were somebody special: you treated all the interviewees with kindness, empathy and care. All interviewees talked about it whilst in the waiting room. That's why I wanted to see you again to get to know more about you. One doesn't meet such people every day!"

◆━━━◆

By this time, Helen was looking down and tears were running down her face. "I don't know what to say, James, but again, thank you very much for the compliment."

The waiter brought the next course, which they, again, ate in silence. When the pudding came, James couldn't help himself: he took a spoonful from his plate and offered it to Helen, saying: "For Helen, the most amazing lady. Please open your mouth, and I'll feed you." Helen reluctantly opened her mouth, and James put the food in her mouth with a broad smile.

As they walked out of the restaurant after the meal, James held Helen's hand and softly said: "I hope you won't mind me taking you out again; I would like to know you better, and hopefully you would want to know more about me too."

"Surely, James, you won't like to know more about me," Helen said in response. "I'm carrying a lot of baggage, which I'm sure you won't want to carry too!"

"I would like to be the judge of that, if you don't mind, young lady," said James. "Can we meet again, please?"

"Can you please give me time to think about it?" asked Helen. "If you give me your phone number, I'll call you to let you know in a few days' time."

"That's fine, Helen, I'll write it down for you when we get back to your office, as I have nothing to write it on now."

At Helen's office, James jotted down his phone number and said: "I hope to hear from you soon. Till then, goodbye." He then left.

Helen was pleased to know that she was still attractive and that a new man could fancy her soon after what she had been through recently. James seemed a very nice and caring man, but she felt that starting a new relationship so soon after Jonathan's death would be a betrayal to his memory, and this would make her very sad and unhappy. She was still coming to terms with the loss of her two previous amazing partners, Steven and Jonathan. Shouldn't she, therefore, tell James that she wasn't ready to get into a new relationship yet? But how would he take it? She thought about this a lot, but she couldn't come to a decision, but she didn't have the guts to say so to him. She, therefore, decided not to phone him.

James waited, and waited for Helen's phone call, but she didn't call. After two months, he couldn't wait any longer and he decided to phone Helen at work. Lucky for him, she was free to answer a personal call.

"Hi, Helen," he said. "I hope you're alright. I've been waiting for your call for quite a long time, but you haven't phoned yet. Is there anything wrong? Please tell me."

"No, James," she replied. "Nothing wrong. It's because of the heavy baggage I mentioned the last time we met. I wouldn't like to burden you with it. I've been thinking very hard about phoning or not phoning you, and I concluded that it would be best for you not to get involved with me. I hope you do understand."

"No, Helen, I don't understand," he said. "The more reason we should meet again soon so that you can tell me about the baggage you're carrying. I'll then be the judge of whether or not to carry it with you! Please give me a chance. Okay?"

Helen kept quiet for some time and then said: "If you insist, James, then yes, we can meet again for a short time, just for me to relate my story. When do you want us to meet?"

"How does next Saturday lunchtime sound to you?" James asked.

"That'll be fine with me," Helen said. "Let's do that, then."

"Done, and thanks a lot, James said. You tell me where you'd like to go; it was my choice last time."

"How about a Spanish Restaurant not far from me? They serve wonderful traditional Spanish dishes I love very much, such as Paella, Patatas Bravas and Tostones, and the staff are extremely friendly. There is also an outside part of the restaurant. Suppose it is a nice sunny day. I would love to have a meal there. I'll text you the address. What do you say?"

"That's fine, Helen," said James. "See you soon then, and goodbye for now."

They met at the Spanish Restaurant which Helen had suggested. It was a typical Spanish Restaurant, in bright Spanish colours of yellow and red. On the walls were hanging pictures depicting Spanish activities, such as bullfighting and Flamenco Dancing. The outside part of the restaurant was beautifully laid out and very inviting. The table Helen had booked was inside the restaurant, by the window, with the sun streaming through.

While they waited to be taken to their table, James suggested that they go for a drink in the Bar area. They were led to a table by the window, and as they sat down, Helen thought: 'Oh, my goodness! This seems a repeat of my first proper meeting with Jonathan! I hope it'll not follow the whole journey through!' They were served their drinks at a table by the window like it was when she and Jonathan went out on their first date. 'How weird this is!' Helen thought.

A Waiter came over to them to let them know that their table was ready, and he led them to it.

During their lunch, James paused and looked into Helen's eyes and cheekily said: "Are you ready to tell me about the heavy baggage you're carrying?"

"I can, but our food will go very cold," Helen replied. "Can't we finish at least this course? It is a very long story!"

"Yah, let's do that, James answered." I don't mind listening to a long story; I'm very intrigued, and I can't wait!"

After the first course, James put down his cutlery and said to Helen:

"I'm very ready to hear your story now, Helen."

Helen, too, put down her cutlery and looked at James. "Right, here we go!" she said.

She calmly and in a quiet voice, related her story, starting from the murder of her first serious boyfriend, and later her fiancé Steven, by Idi Amin's soldiers, her escape from Idi Amin's brutal regime, her stay at the Catholic Convent in Nairobi, Kenya, her flight to the UK and starting a new life there. Before she started her life with Jonathan and its tragic end, she stopped for a while, and tears filled her eyes.

"Jonathan was a special, and a truly amazing, man. Ours was 'love at first sight!" Helen continued with her story. "From the very beginning, he showed me so much kindness and care that he hardly allowed me to do anything for myself. At the start of our relationship, both his parents and my parents knew that ours was a special relationship and that we were meant to be together forever. We shared everything, and I mean everything! That's why I can't believe he's no longer by my side. I feel so lost without him. I know it'll be a very long time for me to accept that he's gone forever." By this time, Helen could hardly speak, and buckets of tears were continuously flowing down her face.

"Oh, Helen, please don't cry," James said as he walked over to her to give her a hug. "You're also bringing tears to my eyes. It's a very powerful story, my dear. But if it's too much for you to tell me the story in one go, you can stop it now, and we'll continue it another time."

"No, James, I'd rather finish it off now," said Helen. "I don't want to get sad again, continuing with the story. "She then wiped away the tears and softly continued her story.

She said that when she met Jonathan, she thought that she had finally found everlasting happiness. But sadly, it was taken away abruptly in a horrendous car crash quite recently. She said that the pain of losing Jonathan was still very raw in her heart. As she'd already lost two wonderful men, both at the height of happiness, she thought it wasn't sensible to get into another relationship, just in case the same thing happened again.

She stopped the story suddenly and went quiet, and she put her hands over her face. James noticed that she was crying again. He got up again, quickly went over to her, and gave her another big hug.

"I'm so sorry, Helen," he said quietly. "It sounds like you've had a very rough time, my dear. But I don't think it's sensible to deny yourself further happiness. I think those horrible days are behind you now. I want you to cheer up, please."

He walked back to his seat and sat down. Looking at her with a smile on his face, he said: "I bet you your next relationship will bring you everlasting happiness. You never know. It could very well be with the person sitting right in front of you!"

Helen opened her eyes widely, and opened her mouth to say something, but nothing came out. Very surprised but with a big smile, she said: "But why do you want to get involved with a person with so much sad baggage? And we hardly know each other!"

I know that." James said, stretching his hand to touch hers. "We have all the time in the world to get to know each other."

"But you haven't even told me about yourself," said Helen. "Since you've heard my gruesome story, am I not entitled to hear your story, too?"

"But, of course," he replied. "Let us finish our meal first, and then I'll tell you, my story. I'm afraid it is quite boring!"

"I can't comment on your suggestion of a relationship until I hear your boring story," Helen said.

"That's fine and very fair," James said. "I'll tell you the boring story right now."

When they finished their meal, they requested that their coffee be served to them in the Bar area. They went to the table they had sat at before, and while they took the coffee, James related his story.

James was born and educated in Bournemouth, and both his parents were Civil Servants. He had one brother and one sister.

For his university education, he chose to go to a university in Michigan, USA where he graduated with an MA degree in Marketing. When he returned to the UK, like his parents, he joined the Civil Service and worked there until two years ago when he opted to go freelance as a Marketing Consultant. That was why he was able to apply for the short-term Marketing Consultancy job at the Company Helen worked for and was posted to their Nairobi branch, which Helen knew already. He was now in the process of applying for more Marketing Consultancy positions elsewhere, and arrangement for the posting were almost finalised; he expected to be posted to The Gambia on another six-month contract.

He was a divorced man with three children: one boy in his twenties and two girls in their teens. He was not in a relationship with anyone at that time, and therefore, he was a free man. At the end of the story, he said "Boring story, isn't it?" He laughed, looking at Helen.

"Not at all, James," Helen answered, "A very interesting story, particularly the last sentence: 'I'm now free!' I would have at least six months to think about everything we've spoken about today and then give you an answer upon your return from The Gambia."

"That's very fair, Helen," James said. "I want you to be completely sure before you get back to me. However, if you decide that it's right for you to go into a relationship with me, I promise it will be a life-long one. You're such an amazing and wonderful lady, and you deserve a great life. Hopefully, it will be true for me too. Let's toss to that, can we?"

"Of course!" said Helen cheerfully, as they raised their coffee cups and together said: "To us and the future!"

They left the restaurant, and James offered to drive Helen back to her house.

The following day, which was a Sunday, Helen decided to drive to her parents-in-law's home in Kent to pay a visit to Jonathan's grave. She stopped at a Florist's shop and bought a lovely bouquet of flowers, mainly in Jonathan's favourite colours, blue and purple, and attached a card on which she inscribed: Darling Jon, I miss you immensely, but before I do anything, I always stop a minute and ask: 'Will JT approve of this?' I know your wisdom supersedes everyone's! Lots of love and kisses, HT.'

She walked alone to Jonathan's grave and stood quietly beside it; her heart heavy yet resolute. As she gazed at the weathered stone, she found herself speaking to him as if he were still there. She shared her reflections on their shared past and the journey she had endured since. It's a moment of bittersweet farewell, where she acknowledges the pain but also expresses her determination to finally move on.

The poignant scene marked the end of her tumultuous journey and signified the beginning of a new chapter in her life.

She placed the flowers on the grave, blew a loving kiss to her late husband, Jonathan, and then solemnly walked back to her car for her journey back to London.

*Join Helen in the next chapter of her extraordinary journey **in the next book** as she navigates through further challenges and the unyielding pursuit of a new beginning.*